THE LAWS

THE LAWS

Connie Palmen

Translated by Richard Huijing

George Braziller
New York

First published in the United States of America
in 1993 by George Braziller, Inc.

First published in Holland in 1990 by
Prometheus Amsterdam under the title *De Wetten*

For information, please address the publisher:

George Braziller, Inc.
60 Madison Avenue
New York, New York 10010

Library of Congress Cataloging-in-Publication Data

Palmen, Connie.
     [Wetten. English]
The laws: a novel / Connie Palmen; translated from the
Dutch by Richard Huijing.
p. cm.
ISBN 0-8076-1329-0
I. Title.
PT5881.26.A46W4813   1993   93-3796
839.3'1364--dc20   CIP

Printed and bound in the United States of America
First U.S. edition 1993

'When I fall, I shall weep with happiness'

Samuel Beckett

THE LAWS

Chapter I

THE ASTROLOGER

I first met the astrologer in the summer of 1980. It was on a Friday the thirteenth. I notice such things only afterwards. A Friday the thirteenth can pass like any other day but when all kinds of things crop up and it turns into a day full of events, it is nevertheless as if the name and the number have a secret treaty and it is only due to your own conceit that you dare to disregard the pointers of fate.

Since the beginning of my student years I had worked every Friday afternoon in a remainder bookshop in the Pijp. It was quiet there and I was able to read a book in peace, or leaf through the daily papers. I never read the papers, I just leaf through them. Real news is sufficiently served by the headlines, and the history of news is always old and well known.

More often than not, I would write a letter to some old acquaintance or other. So, too, now.

It was a warm day, the rack with newspapers stood outside and the door was open. Inaudibly, someone had come inside, a small, thickset man with a full beard and a pair of those half-sized specs. It annoyed me that I didn't know whether he had been standing there for a long time, looking at me like that, head cocked and peering with a probing look over the rims of his glasses, something that causes such a horrible amount of the white of someone's eyes to be visible.

I don't need to see that much of the white of someone's eyes.

From the extent of my resentment, I concluded for the first time that day that I was in a bad mood and preferred to see no one. Peace around me, gob shut, not a word.

I said a friendly word of welcome and bent over my letter again. Now it was especially a matter of preventing the sentence in my head from expanding into a monotonous litany. Should I continue to repeat 'Don't stand there gawping at me, you jack-ass,' I would only dupe myself, for I can whip myself up into great emotion without anyone being aware of it.

I re-read the last lines of my letter. Without leaving a line of blank space, I went on and wrote:

'Now all of a sudden there's an ass standing in the middle of the shop. You know I can't handle animals. What am I to do with an ass?'

This helped.

He walked through the shop. His gait was a strange one, more of a shuffle. When you have worked in a shop for a while you learn to keep an eye on people without them knowing they're being spied upon. You keep them stored constantly in the corner of your eye, like a shadow, and soon you quickly recognise any unusual movements.

Theft was quite the last thing I suspected him of. That hesitant, crooked gait was more that of a timid animal than of someone who was mustering courage in order to strike. When he halted and stood in front of a rack or a table I felt that he was looking at me, thoughtfully and enquiringly, as if he was wondering where he had seen me before.

I have a good memory for faces. I had never seen

2

him before.

The moment you suspect danger somewhere, you do best to look the enemy straight in the eye. If you avert your gaze from something you're afraid of, your fear multiplies a thousandfold and also stays with you much longer than necessary. Instinctively, you avoid that. It's just the same as riding a motorbike. Riding pillion, when taking a corner, you are inclined to move your body against the bend, keeping it as far as possible away from the asphalt, but in fact you must go along with it, throw your entire body into the bend until your nose whizzes along the road surface, nearly touching it. You must do the thing you fear, for that's the safest.

I looked up, straight into his face, and I asked him whether I might be of service. This unnerved him badly, the question did. His body gained mobility to an unexpectedly great degree and he shook his head irascibly.

'Oh no, no,' he said, as if he was gasping for breath.

So much shyness is unbearable to witness, so I smiled in order to put him at ease. Down, down boy, it's all right.

Nervous people can suddenly become very aggressive. I wanted to get on with that letter.

'Well, ehm . . . perhaps,' he stammered. A few weeks ago he had been walking through this area too and then, in some bookshop or other – he thought it was this one, but he wasn't sure, somewhere in the Pijp, in any case – in a shop window, he had seen a book about Vincent Van Gogh. It was this he was looking for. Not because he liked Van Gogh, for that matter, no, on the contrary: precisely *because* the thing he couldn't understand in himself was why he had something against Van Gogh, did he want to read the book.

He spoke quickly but very softly. It was a muttering with little air and in an accent I could not place. But then I hardly ever can.

3

'If we do have it, it would have to be over there,' I said and pointed to the shelves to the left of the table at which I was sitting.

'Ah, yes, quite,' he said and looked obligingly in the direction I pointed out to him, then cast a few questioning glances at me and continued to stand there, dawdling.

What did he want? His tale had sounded strange but before you knew it you might end up having a chinwag with all and sundry about the pros and cons of Vincent Van Gogh, and I really didn't feel like that.

With his back bent, he walked past my table. As he passed, I scented an arid smell. He was now standing a metre away from me with his face turned towards the shelves with books on Art.

'Sagittarius-Scorpio,' he said.

Correct.

He was so used to it. During a first encounter, he would run into a wall of resistance, as if there was something wrong with him, something strange, no, worse: something repulsive. He wasn't blind, was he? He could see it, couldn't he? He saw it in their eyes, by the features on their faces, the muscles around their mouths – all indicated rejection. The moment he told them what they were, their entire attitude changed. It would be strange indeed if then something wouldn't light up in those eyes and a glowing haze of curiosity would take up arms against the clear hardness of the first glance.

A hole in one! The astrologer read the preparedness in my face, could abandon the last remnant of pretended desire to buy and he stepped up to my table. Along with his physical body, a compact scent came my way, the smell of a dusty, dessicated corpse.

'Fifty-five?' he asked.

I nodded, surprised, and in my turn asked the question

4

how he knew all this, out of nothing like that. He said it wasn't a knowing but a way of looking. The colour of my clothing, the moon-shaped lines of my face and '*le petit grain de folie dans tes yeux*'.

'And that's it,' he said and pointed at the table top.

'What is?'

'Writing,' he replied.

Bullseye! Come what may, I have done an about-turn and decide to leave them be for what they are, the newspaper, the books and the letter. Demonstratively, I push all the paperwork aside in order to make it clear to the stranger that I will listen to him for as long as it takes until I know everything about this way of looking and judging, about what is written in the stars, about something which I want to have been written down somewhere and which will prove to be inescapable: the connection between myself, as a Sagittarius-Scorpio if needs be, and writing.

From his shoulder hung a bag made out of cheap material, crammed full. He put the bag down on the floor and brought out a fat, oblong book. By the look of it, it had been brought out quite a few times before from sloppy bags and used often. The linen spine was torn at the ends and in several places scraps of paper protruded from the pages.

'Now then, let's have a look at your odds and sods,' he said, after I had informed him about the place and the hour of my birth. He was beginning to amuse me. I thought that a fun way of putting it: your odds and sods.

He was on his home territory and he was powerful. His face had now acquired something cheerful and free about it and it was much better like that. If you have someone opposite you who only nods, bows and is obsequious, you run out of things to say in no time and you are so bored to

5

death that it doesn't even turn you hot or cold when someone tells you, for instance, that in a previous existence you were none other than Mata Hari and that he will provide you with convincing proof of this fact.

There were only charts in the book. He asked for a sheet of paper and a pen. He leafed back and forth, ran his finger down the charts and jotted down a number of symbols on the sheet of paper. At times he would groan something like 'Oh, la la,' or 'Dear, dear, dear,' and would look at me so mischievously, as if I was also in the know as to what it was about and for years had kept a sin from him of which he had finally caught the scent.

Meanwhile, there were a few people in the shop and I was obliged to divide my attention between the customers and the man opposite me. He saw all kinds of numbers and signs and those numbers and signs again meant something different, something about me, something that made him groan, surprised him, which made him say things like 'What a theme!' and 'Again a triangle!' His remarks contained a promise, a story about myself that I was about to hear, any time now.

'*Voilà*, your cosmic brand,' he said at a certain moment and shoved a sheet covered in scribbles under my nose.

This is what it contained:

$$\odot \; 2° \nearrow \quad \mathrm{D} \; 4° \; \Upsilon \quad \lessgtr \; 27° \; \mathrm{m} \quad \female \; 25° \nearrow$$

$$\male \; 28° \triangleq \quad 4 \; 0° \; \mathrm{mp} \quad \hbar \; 25° \; \mathrm{m} \quad \mathrm{H} \; 2° \; \Omega$$

$$\female \; 29° \triangleq \quad \mathrm{P} \; 29° \; \Omega \quad \mathit{asc}. \; 30° \; \mathrm{m}$$

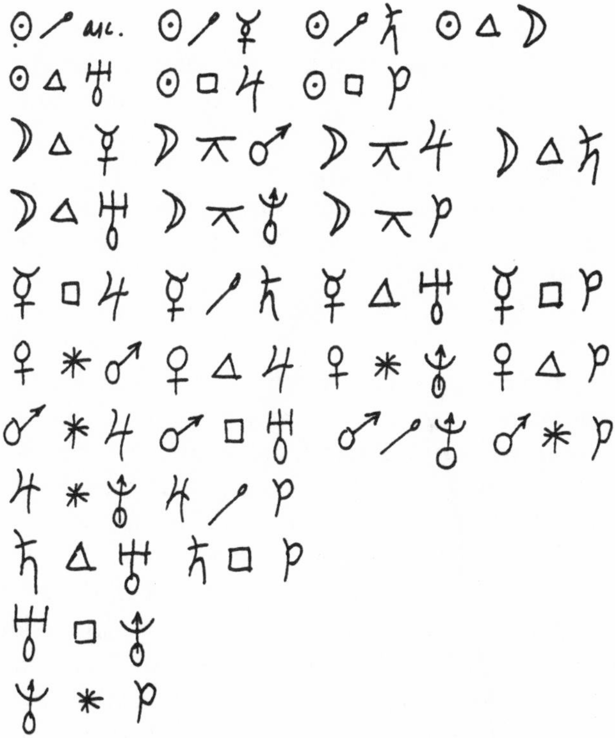

☉ ⚹ ♀ uc. ☉ ⚹ ☿ ☉ ⚹ ♄ ☉ △ ☽

☉ △ ♅ ☉ □ ♃ ☉ □ ♀

☽ △ ♀ ☽ ⊼ ♂ ☽ ⊼ ♃ ☽ △ ♄

☽ △ ♅ ☽ ⊼ ☿ ☽ ⊼ ♀

☿ □ ♃ ☿ ⚹ ♄ ☿ △ ♅ ☿ □ ♀

♀ ✳ ♂ ♀ △ ♃ ♀ ✳ ☿ ♀ △ ♀

♂ ✳ ♃ ♂ □ ♅ ♂ ⚹ ☿ ♂ ✳ ♀

♃ ✳ ☿ ♃ ⚹ ♀

♄ △ ♅ ♄ □ ♀

♅ □ ☿

☿ ✳ ♀

I myself couldn't read it either.

Venus, Mars and the Moon I could still recognise, but what in heaven's name did they represent? Which signs had caused his exclamations and why? Which words were now in his head and how did they get there?

The paper bore a tale about myself but in a code that was unreadable to me. This is frustrating.

He possessed a text which contained precisely how I was made up, which were my good characteristics and which my bad, and whether I was predestined to do great deeds or whether I might better pack it in right now and turn the nightmare of a banal life into a dream at last. I felt robbed.

He had something that was mine but I myself had no access to my own tale.

Disappointed, but careful, I said that this was secret code to me and asked him to put everything into plain language so I myself might also be able to read who I was, if you please.

'Oh, la la,' he said again and laughed like someone who sees his suspicions confirmed, 'you're quite a demanding little lady, my-oh-my.'

'Where does it say that?' I managed to ask.

He wouldn't attempt a translation into everyday language. He had noted down the degrees and aspects, but each astrologer would interpret those relations between the planets differently. In order to accommodate me, he wrote above and below the signs what they stood for, which was the Moon and which the Sun and by what symbols the eight planets were represented, the names of the aspects and what the names were of the twelve signs of the Zodiac.

From the moment he had the book of charts in his hands, a bold directness had crept into the way he addressed me. I began to wonder who he was, where he came from, what he kept himself occupied with, how old he was, and what this thing of his was with Van Gogh.

However, I know myself. As like as not, the person opposite me will only be talking about himself, and though I gladly submerge myself in the tales of other people and have difficulty in getting round to talking about myself, things were different this time. Opposite me stood the author of the tale about myself, a messenger of the gods, and mine was only the duty to listen. My story was with him and I could get to hear it if I was able to suppress my curiosity as to his life and could keep check on the ridiculous politeness of enquiring in interested tones as to what-all had happened to him and what marks had been branded on to him, those of the stars in heaven or of life on the streets.

To know what you want is power and power makes one honest. My aim was to get the story about myself out into the open, before closing time. After that I would think again. So I told him that, though indeed I could now read 'Sun-trine-Moon', I knew no more than when even that was unreadable.

'You are a philosophical whore-angel,' he said, chuckling.

Then I offered him a chair and asked whether he felt like some coffee.

'The theme is a splendid one. It rattles, it's heavy and a bit bizarre, too, but in essence it's very harmoniously made. It is all right. Your theme is ruled completely by Saturn, and Saturn's no easy planet. But in your case, the difficulty is obviated by other planets. When Saturn dominates a theme, this brings much melancholy in its wake, for it is the sign of melancholiacs. But you are morbid in a rather exuberant way. In your case, melancholy springs forth more from having knowledge and allowing your mind to work than from mystery as is usually the case with Sagittarians. Your pleasure lies embedded in your pretty little head, in learning. Passion is in your case the passion of the mind. That's what a philosophical whore-angel is. You barter with the most precious part of yourself: you sell your soul for a little knowledge. The more opportunity you get to have your brain run at top speed, the happier and more grateful you are. Thinking relaxes you. Saturn loves order and you are not satisfied until you have placed everything in a scheme or a structure. If the outcome of all the fretful pondering and ordering is melancholy, then you'll live with it. Anything is better than having no name for things.

9

'It's very bizarre, but you have no oppositions. I know many themes but it's for the first time in my life that I see a theme without oppositions. Perhaps I have made a mistake,' he said and he ran his hand through his beard, 'it's possible. I'll check up on it back home. Everybody has at least one opposition, so why don't you? And you have ten trines, no less, another impossible quantity. Ten! The trine is the triangle and a most harmonious aspect, for then it's always a case of arbitration between extremes. You're a real lucky lady. Your Sun stands in a fine triangulation to your Moon and Venus triangulates with Pluto. That is very good. It's also quite pleasant for me for, like this, you are very sympathetic to my Mars and Sun. If there's any personal profit in it for me is still an open question, for with a Venus such as yours you are the friend of all men. You are a boon to them. Oh indeed, you do kick them with those nasty Piscean feet of yours, but afterwards you lick their wounds.

'Yes, you're anything but an easy woman. You have your deadly aspects. Saturn squared with Pluto makes people very fierce, but with you that hard Pluto is sheltered securely with your Venus. This'll give you unbelievably fierce little ladies but, because they think it's right, they destroy out of love, really. Destruction and construction are two important aspects in your theme. It is suffused with death, it's riddled with Scorpios there. Moreover, you also have Saturn in your ascendant for good measure, in Scorpio itself, that is.

'It's most fascinating. In fact, you're only out for one thing: you want to peel off the appearance of everything and get down to the soul of people and of things. That's what you're out for: possession of the soul.'

'And what about writing then?' I asked.

'Oh, it's in your theme everywhere,' he said, 'spoilt for choice. First, let's take a look at Mercury. Mercury is

Hermes, the god of scripture, but a thing like that you know too, of course. Hermes behaves very chameleon-like. He himself only becomes somebody when there is somebody else present, a personality to which he can bring order or one he can replace – how should I put it? Hermes assumes the shape of all that he finds in the other, of the persons which make up someone, and then he starts to structure or he begins to analyse that little lot really thoroughly, so that it becomes clear. If you're empty and there's nothing to you, then there's nothing for Hermes to do, either. But in your case he has his hands full, with someone having a receptive Moon like yours. You are very susceptible to impressions and what ends up in your noddle has to be digested in some way or other, for if you don't digest or process your impressions, they disappear as if you had never had them. And you can't stand that. By the way Hermes is placed within a theme, it is easy to read how the digesting of impressions takes place and how someone handles the results of all his analyses, how someone attempts to convey to others what learning has produced.

'With you, Mercury is placed at the rear in the sign of Scorpio and he's in your twelfth house. The twelfth house is the house of hidden knowing, the hiding place of the secret. When you have Hermes in the house of the secret and thus in the house where you hide yourself most and are lonely there, then it might be that you are also not able to convey your discoveries and your knowledge directly to other people. For most people, the twelfth house is a horrible house, but that which is frightening to one can be indispensable to a writer. You have to be alone in order to be able to think about the world, but you even have to be alone in order to be able to make contact with others, in order to allow them to profit by your knowledge. D'you understand? You simply have to find a solution for the

11

way in which you can communicate with others and convey your messages without actually having to deal with those others – physically, I mean.

'And here there might indeed be a problem for you. In your theme, there are also so many aspects which precisely drive you into the arms of others, while those others are just the ones that keep you from what you need, from where your happiness may lie.'

Though I had never dragged a Hermes, a Saturn, a few Scorpios or a twelfth house of hidden suffering into the proceedings, that which the astrologer said sounded unbelievably true to my ears.

The most irksome thing about thinking, in my opinion, is that so often you end up with paradox. Writing, for instance, seems to have something to do with a paradoxical desire. Whatever it may be that you wish to achieve, be it love, solace, understanding or meaning, in order to have your way you must in fact keep yourself as far as possible from others and withdraw completely; this, while the only thing you ultimately desire is a thing you can only obtain from others. It is a cumbersome attempt to make someone else understand something of that which you think is the truth, but which you cannot possibly utter when you also happen to be forced to look into someone's face as well. At that moment, so much new truth is added on top. But there's worse to come: things are not sweetness and light between writing and truth. This you find out soon enough when, finally, you have put up enough resistance to the suction power of the world and, having dawdled for ever and a day, you finally end up on your tod at the writing table. So there you are and you want so badly to be honest and do that which always fails under the observing eye of the world. Being honest is very difficult. When you write, you think you are troubled less by this, as you have manfully freed yourself from the eyes, ears and the voice of the people who cause you to lie and cause you time and again to do and say that which you actually never wished to do, to say. You sit quietly and write, you write down everything according to the truth; you re-read sentences and discover to your marked dismay that the truth is writ as though it were a great lie, worse than everyday lies and ugly to boot. This is why many people write but few become writers. Most chuck it in at this stage. But then, it's an affront. No human being will keep it up, filling pages with lines that make you nauseous with revulsion and, when it comes down to it, are unreadable. If you want to continue, you will have to start lying again afresh. The desire for truth remains the same, but the real art is to speak the truth by lying about it.

I didn't dare ask the astrologer whether I stood a chance of success.

He looked at me, his eyes beaming. His story was having an effect. I was excited, surprised, cheerful and I was grateful to him. This was why I wanted to do something in return, and I told him how correct it was what he said, that I studied philosophy, liked to write, was a structure-maniac and that I could also manage to imagine something in relation to the word whore-angel.

The only thing that was still giving me a headache was how I was to remember who I was according to a version in which Saturn, Hermes and the twelfth house were featured.

'I could also take a look at what is going on in your ninth house, too,' the astrologer said, urged on by my enthusiasm. 'It is both the house of philosophy as well as that of publicity. So you see, you *are* a lucky little lady,' he said and he pointed out a number of the signs in succession.

13

'Jupiter and Pluto are together in the ninth house. Jupiter is on home ground in the ninth house and a thing like that always reinforces the whole shebang. The god is at home, should I say? No wonder you want to be published and that you study philosophy. Although, perhaps it's actually a waste of time and you might as well have stayed away from university. Going by this brand, you have always been a philosopher. Look, Sagittarius is the lord of the ninth house and he himself is the philosopher among the signs. When, like you do, you have the Sun in your first house, the point in question is why you are dawdling about like this. You have known for ages. You have Pluto in Leo and your Leo is ruled by the Sun and your sun-sign is Sagittarius, d'you see?'

'No.'

And I didn't. I felt he was going to say something important, something I was desperately eager to hear, but something I also thought terrible.

'Someone with the Sun in the first house knows from the day of his birth who he is. All kinds of things can go wrong, but that realisation is there. A philosophy sign in the first house, a cocksure Pluto who is working on your Sun with all his energy and then the philosopher among the planets in his own house to boot, well, you're bound to. Your Sun is your personality and you were born very personally indeed. Everything points really in one direction only. Why don't you take it as it comes? I wish I had so much luck. Probably Saturn is bothering you more than I thought and he's slowing the whole thing down. So much luck, free of charge, has to be put to the test, otherwise you become lazy and apathetic. I don't know, y'know. I, too, am only reading what's put there.'

Moods are treacherous. My initial excitement had disappeared. Suddenly my heart was heavy. Why was I sitting here, swallowing stories about myself like a hungry

14

wolf, while my first design was crystal clear? Why wasn't I able to stay at home, behind my table, in order to write, if this had been on the cards right from the beginning? Why hadn't I continued to be who I was and gone straight for my target without turning off down all those strange side-roads, so that I only got into a muddle and fancied that I was becoming richer while it boiled down to the fact that I was losing ever more? What, for a few lousy cents, was I doing in a bookshop in the Pijp, wasting my precious time listening to some dotty nonsense or other coming from some kind of lonely eccentric, nonsense about the stars in heaven, while actually I knew better and didn't really believe in anything?

'What on earth am I meant to do with this?' I burst forth to the astrologer. 'Again, everything is possible but when it comes down to it, you yourself must want it all, do it yourself and you must choose for something. No excuses. Sounds too good to be true to me. It sounds like the deception of youth. Then you still think that everything happens of its own accord and that you don't have to lift a finger for anything.'

Youth is a deceptive affair. In your youth, life appears to be a tame animal that stretches out at your feet, and a few measly pettings from you will do for it to remain eternally faithful to you.

At fourteen, I had a dream. I was going down a street in my village and detected great excitement among the people the moment I passed by them. They waved and gave me friendly nods, benevolently and yet with respect. Then they would put their heads together and be talking about me. There was something about me, but I didn't know what. Having become curious, I ran back home. My mother always knew everything.

The kitchen door is open and my mother is standing in

15

front of me, flanked by my brothers. She looks at me and claps her hands together. Surprised, she asks me if I really don't know yet myself. No, no, I haven't a clue.

It had been announced on the radio not yet an hour ago: I had won the Nobel Prize. That could not possibly be true. I had not published a word yet.

'They know you're a writer,' my mother says, 'and do nothing but, all day. 'They're giving you the prize in advance because they know that it's good.'

That's what I mean, see. That's the kind of thing I call the deception of youth. When you're young you quite simply cannot imagine that you yourself must bring about whatever it is you badly want to have or want to be. You think it's sufficient to want something passionately. In your youth everything happens, just like that, and you take it as it comes, the good and the bad. One day it comes to you with some violence that the desire is a condition, but one insufficient for the life you wish to lead. The desire has the tendency to skip things and then it becomes a dream. It focuses on the consequences and unimportant side-issues of what you can do. Thus, hardly anyone sees being a filmstar as a profession, yet everybody would like to be one. The desire, however, does not focus on the work, the heat of lights, the petty-minded other filmstars, the jealousy and the boredom on the set. The thing desired is the adulation that befalls the filmstars, an adulation like the one they themselves feel when they see somebody on the screen. In fact they long most for themselves to be someone who is longed for in equal measure to the way they themselves long for an idol. No one gladly confronts the reality of the stars.

Youth ends with the realisation of the necessity and the beauty of work, of the reality of work, never mind the final results, if need be, but preferably not.

If you insist on wanting to be a writer then you must

16

write books – that's what it boils down to.

Suddenly the astrologer looked defeated.
  'I'm sorry I raised my voice like that,' I said.
  With a fluttering hand he waved away my objections.
'Doesn't matter,' he said, directing his eyes toward the
paper, 'it's your Mars. You bear the brand of a child of the
gods, but the divine makes you angry.'
  'You just tell me a bit more about the obstacles and the
trying things,' I said.
  Something had to be the cause of it, surely.
  'Ah, to you even tragedy is a trifle,' the astrologer said,
relieved. 'Actually, all of it's too neat, really. With just
harmony in your theme, you won't get down to anything.
You need a few hard aspects in order to be able to grow
and to prove yourself. You have a number of non-
conjunctions, so you'll get your way. According to some
astrologers, the non-conjunction is the gravest aspect
within the entire horoscope. In your case, the non-
conjunctions are all made with your Moon. The Moon is
the feminine, is feeling, and in your case there's a lot of
pain there. The Moon is your heart and your heart is being
bombarded by Mars, Jupiter, Neptune and by Pluto on top
of all that, I now see. It is indeed a lot and no fun. When
your Moon makes such a hard aspect with Jupiter, for
instance, you demand more goodness, beauty and truth
from life than is, perhaps, available. You think that it
exists in the measure to which you seek it and you expect,
you might say, to discover it somewhere every day, but all
the while you do not find it. That makes you furious. This
is why you are a destroyer, too. You have Scorpio in the
house of Mercury and then you have Saturn in your
Scorpio as well. That means that your strength lies in the
destruction of things the way they are, in order to make
something new from the fragments. This is why someone

17

like you, with your Mars at 150 degrees to your Moon, is
unpredictable, alternately hard and soft, volatile, easily
hurt. You have many double signs in aspects: the Moon,
who pops up time and again in different guises; Sagittarius, who is earthly and heavenly at once and opposite
Gemini; and, moreover, you have a split Pluto in hard
aspect to your Moon. When you also have your Sun at
right angles to your Pluto, you transform so much that in
the end you yourself don't know any longer what it's all
about. But that wild Pluto aspects nicely with your Venus
and with all his plutonian energy he's in the house of
publicity. So, you'll be making quite a muddle there, there
on the spot where you are with your feeling and where you
wish to make your name.'

'Thank you,' I said, for I was grateful.

He raised his hand and drew a circle in the air above his
head.

'You haven't gained it from me,' he said, shyly, 'it was
already writ.'

It was past closing time and I hadn't noticed. I listened,
though I do wonder whether the mixed condition of
anaesthesia and excitement merits the name of listening.
Some or other specialist, connoisseur, professor or moral-
ist has pronounced about more or less everything in the
world, how it is meant to be in its most optimal form.
Good listening demands empathy and the casting aside of
prejudices. Laws like those: I have always been very
susceptible to them. When I had read only a few books, I
always remembered with the greatest possible ease the
laws for every form of good behaviour, the correct mode
of presentation, the right way to act. Without laws, I did
not know what to do with myself. Nor did the others, or so
I still thought then. The difficulties appeared when I
started to read more books and discovered there were

several laws concerning the same topic, differing ones, too. Things became tragic indeed, mind you, when I cottoned on to the fact that, though the others had laws in their heads, they rarely or never read books. They got them from somewhere else. I was stumped as to where. Some people seem to have the laws in them, innately. They haven't read books and yet they have an opinion, a conviction, an idea as to how the world is meant to tick. They are convinced of their own right and they don't need to look up the way they are to think about something, not anywhere.

I didn't understand how this could be. I was frightened that I didn't have a nature. At best, I had had one at one time, but I had lost it, somewhere, on the way.

To listen the way I had been listening to the astrologer that afternoon in any case had little more to do with empathy for someone else's story. This story was about me and it was eighty per cent incomprehensible. Entire chunks of sentences were unintelligible to me. Yet I listened. Embedded among the afflicts, sextiles and conjunctions of the descending sign on the trine of the first house, glinted the astrologer's wilful idiom. He only sounded me out as to whether I understood what he said when employing a French expression for which he could not find a Dutch equivalent just at that moment, or when he wished, by means of a metaphor, to indicate the effects of planetary aspects on my actions. He never did this when talking about the calculations which were truly incomprehensible to me.

The following Friday, five minutes after I had unlocked the front door to the shop, he was standing on the doorstep. He dawdled as he came in, looked apologetic, and tensely scrutinised my face. I suspected him of having waited in a café until I had come cycling round the corner and had barely been able to muster enough patience to drink up his cup of coffee.

Just like at our first meeting, I was beset by a feeling of irritation when I saw him. This surprised me, for the week before I had relished his stories and he had been so generous with his old-fashioned knowledge. What was it? Was it that hang-dog quality in his attitude, an animal emanation of weakness, humility, dependence?

In the ensuing years, during which I saw him regularly and on one occasion even travelled with him to Paris, I also saw this in the few friends he introduced me to, even in the women with whom he did love, as he called it. Even if it was only for a fraction of a second, when they saw him again, they all at first had something in their eyes as if to fend him off. I blamed myself for doing this, and I have reproached myself hundreds of times later on, but it would not be controlled. I could not get used to it and it never went away. The astrologer's life seemed unpleasant to me. I couldn't understand how he kept it up for so long. Even his nearest and dearest continued to be people who had to be conquered afresh each time, and acquaintance of years' standing retained that clumsy angularity of a first reconnaissance. Only when I met his mother did I understand a little better.

The astrologer had recently moved into a new apartment and his mother would be visiting him there. I had then known him for some two years, but at times I wouldn't see him for months as he would then be staying in France – somewhere. He did not leave an address. On occasion, he would send a picture postcard or a short letter. He called me *Monsieur Lune*. According to him, I looked like a Rubens-woman in soldiers' clothing, which was logical to him as my Moon was wrestling with my Mars. With regard to myself, nothing has ever seemed logical to me and, moreover, I take pleasure in letting as many theories, ideas and thoughts have a go at whatever problem there may be.

Indeed, I have thought about the men-and-women thing but I cannot possibly see it in a simple manner. Just you start with Adam and Eve. Then the issue turns out to be not so much one of whether they get on well and care enough for one another, but that an undefined happiness is disturbed by something entirely different, a third entity, a devil in a convenient disguise, a God who sticks his nose in everywhere – though specifically not with that devil, of course – through the stealing of the knowledge and by it being precisely Eve who allows herself to be seduced into eating something she is not allowed to eat at all, thus violating the law and in her turn seducing Adam to join in. The more things get added on, the happier I am. When I am able to connect the relationship between men and women with the relationship between God and the devil, knowledge and primal sin, then I won't neglect to do so. Together with the astrologer, a Sun and a Moon joined in and I thought that was fine with me: it stimulated my imagination. I wouldn't be able to make do with just the Sun and the Moon.

The astrologer *was* able to do this and, frankly, it reassured me that this enormous reduction of perspective did not make his life any the more transparent or simple because of it.

Whenever the astrologer returned to the Netherlands ('Holland' he would say) after travelling abroad, he would look me up immediately. He would always bring me something, one or several books and a piece of cheese or a dried sausage with garlic. Everything was wrapped in a brown paper bag on which he had written in felt-tip pen 'Fodder for Monsieur Lune'. The first few days after his

21

return there would be no handling him. He would complain about the coldness and invulnerability (*'ils ne sont pas tactiles'*) of the Dutch, the impossibility of having true contact with anybody here, about the *difference* between here and there. The moment he passed the frontier, Holland jumped on his back and he would have the feeling of lugging something heavy along with him, something that pressed him down and because of which he was barely able to walk upright and had difficulty in breathing. He cried more and more frequently.

From his descriptions of life there, life with the French he had got to know on his travels, an image of the sixties would always pop up in my mind. I have an intuitive aversion to it. I see the sixties as the Middle Ages of the twentieth century, though this image is as intuitive as is my aversion. The Middle Ages are the Middle Ages, and there they are in the right place in history. When the Middle Ages turn up in the twentieth century, time has been snatched from its place and something unreal, something false is happening, an illicit repetition, you might say. That's what it is, according to me. The sixties give me the impression of being untrue, a phoney scene in the stage play of time. This untruth was an intoxication and everybody lived in the stirring compulsion of the lie. This lie was the denial of the twentieth century and it penetrated the bodies, the gestures, the relationships and particularly it penetrated the skin of the language.

I sometimes used to say to the astrologer that he belonged in the Middle Ages. At that time, he would have been able to roam the streets and he would have found shelter everywhere because he had knowledge of the stars and would have been able to predict for the people whether they must harvest today or tomorrow and how many boys and girls were yet to be born. Then people believed such things in a different way than now. He would have had food and would have been free to stay for as long as he wished, for he was a friendly man, after all, and in the past people much more easily took the idiosyncrasies of travelling folk in their stride.

I don't know whether it would have made any difference to the astrologer.

At times, I think it would.

He had requested me to come up to his house, preferably in more than enough time before his mother was due to arrive. I was there with time to spare and handed him the apple pie which I had baked for the occasion. With a nonchalance unusual for him, he took the tart from my hands and put it on the draining board. He was very nervous.

His room was full of cardboard removal boxes. On the stove stood a pan of soup. He had just come out of the shower and had combed his wet hair in a side parting. This made him look like a schoolboy. I suddenly felt sorry for him and laid my hand on his forearm. Something began to churn inside him. He swallowed fiercely. It was as if chunks of compacted air were slamming into a shield behind his rib-cage. With his left hand, he grabbed for my shoulder while clasping the right in front of his mouth from which a long, stretched-out, raw sound came forth.

'I won't manage it,' he groaned, 'I won't manage it. She wins.'

'What won't you manage?' I whispered, for I was afraid.

'October.'

'What's up in October?'

'Then things will look a little brighter for me.' He was breathing with difficulty and told me something about shifts in the firmament, propitious planetary positions, blockades that had been removed and energy to be set free.

'If only I had your Mars. Mine is hopelessly in tatters.

23

All I can do is get furious with the shades. I can only murder my enemies when they are stone dead of their own accord. Sometimes I fantasise about digging up my father from the soil and stabbing him to shreds even now. It's terrible; I wait for my mother's death so that I can crush her. At least you destroy while still alive, so it's still worth the doing that way. As things are now, I don't get ahead by a single inch and all the while my life passes by. But for as long as my mother lives, there is no place for mine, too; it simply cannot take place. That's how it is; I see it in our themes. One of us has to disappear, either she or I. And she has the greater stamina.'

He had started to sound increasingly grim and he saw that I was shaken by this and didn't know what to say. He took my hand and squeezed it.

'I do everything as it's meant to be done, don't I? I walk around, I look, I do the shopping in the shops, I talk about the simple things with the people on the streets, and about the difficult ones with people like you, but it's still as if life passes me by, as if I have nothing to do with it, d'you understand? It's my own life, yet I don't consume it.'

It was impossible for me to bring up flight from reality, mother and father complexes, Oedipus and the entire arsenal of explanations which sometimes you will trot out to someone else in order to cast some light on the matter: not to the astrologer. He had draped a fabric across the world and the knots in the fabric had to do with the heavens, with stars, degrees and numbers. He had incorporated himself in this fabric and were I to tug at one of the threads, the fabric would tear in holes and insanity would slip out on all sides through the mesh of the net.

Half an hour later, his mother rang at the door. She was a small, tawny woman with straight, dead-white hair. She was already in her late seventies but had the rosy-cheeked face of a young girl.

24

The astrologer awaited her by the door and then I saw it. She had it, too.

She greeted him unwillingly as if she herself was surprised ever to have given birth and suck to this fifty-year-old. The look in the eyes of us, his friends, was the look with which he had always been regarded. He was unable to meet any gaze other than this. He sought it. But, Christ, she was his mother.

He managed to make it to October that year and, in that month, he left for France for an indefinite period, trusting in a few changes, the nature of which he didn't know but which he believed to be good for him. Around Christmas, I received a letter from him.

Arles, 19 December 1982

Cher Monsieur Lune,

It has turned out differently than I expected, after all. I do feel that much has happened and for a moment it did indeed look as if things would go better for me, for I was more active and I met nice people. But it's still there, that something that is always there, inside me, in bud, embryonic, and which quietly bides its time and pops up in the course of whatever I may undertake and then destroys what is valuable to me. My happiness is worm-eaten. *Coûte que coûte*, the worm has to go, swept away. But how? *Et quand?* It's in my theme. Never a grip; in everything this grinding.

How are you? *Ça va?* You, too, are alone but you relish it. I don't. You have locked yourself away with the greatest critic of yourself (☉ ⁄ ♄), but I carry a self-destroyer along with me. Keep faith.

It is pretty here. Snow. Bon Noël. Je t'embrasse.
Moi.

I saw him again in spring. He would only be staying in the Netherlands for about three weeks or so, for in France he was busy with something grand. He was playing in the lotto and had designed a system by means of which he could predict which numbers he needed to fill in to scoop the big prize. In order to make the system perfectly watertight, he needed a magazine in which the lucky numbers were noted each week.

He was excited about it. He cast dice at home for hours at a stretch and made long series of figures. It was the first time, he said, that he was able to stay in his house for longer than three hours.

Concentration is beneficial and every time he visited me I would give him the birth date of someone I had just encountered. I now had that story about myself down on paper and my curiosity with regard to my own theme had paled. Besides, I had discovered that the astrologer had a particular eye for a possible combining of our horoscopes. According to him, our planets were in a most advantageous position with regard to one another and it was only my Mars-Neptune-conjunction that provided an obstacle to a possible relationship. As far as I was concerned, there was quite a bit more blocking the way, but I didn't feel like discussing this with him.

When the astrologer met someone, he would at once ask that person for the requisite details. At home, he would then check if there was anything worth his while in the offing. The thing he would like to discover most of all was a theme that seamlessly matched his, the perfect combination of two sets of adventures in which the deficiencies were mutually supplemented and the hubris mutually tempered. Relationships were his speciality.

When he visited, I would at times make known to him that I had no time for him, but if I did let him in, I made sure that he continued to have the floor. He would always provoke new ideas in me, would make connections which I myself would not have arrived at that quickly and he took all his imagery from the gods and goddesses which I, in my turn, found suitable to relate to something I was absorbed in at the time. There is no better way of getting to know myths than through someone to whom they are still a living part of reality.

This is how, by and by, the people with whom I consorted for a longer or shorter period also acquired the quality of characters in the always quite extraordinary tales of the astrologer. I gave him the co-ordinates and he painted the landscape of their starry firmament. Professor De Waeterlinck, Daniel Daalmeyer and Clemens Brandt were conjured up by the astrologer without him ever having met them, nor would he ever come to meet them later.

At times, I try to imagine what it must have looked like inside his head. This is no habit of mine, for in the case of most other people the thought wouldn't cross my mind. In the astrologer's case it did. When he was seeking an explanation for something or acceded to my request to have a look at the state of the heavens when someone or other was born, he would turn his eyes upward, and then it would be as if he wished to roll them inward completely so that they were able to look at a slide-screen inside his head, one on which always the same drawing would appear: a circle.

The circle is divided, like a pie, into twelve pieces. In the tips of the triangles thus formed there are figures. Around and inside the circle appears an endlessly varying series of signs and numbers. The signs are the stars and they have always been in motion and each day they move ever onward. The astrologer was able effortlessly to bring the revolving wheel to a halt and to project from memory a circle on to the screen which depicted the heavens as they appeared on, let's say, December 25th, 1934, at midnight.

According to the biographies, on December 25th, 1934, at midnight, Lucas Anbeek was born, and the astrologer said that one day we would meet, would tear each other's clothes, and that I would lose my plumes.

He turned out to be right about this.

His second visit happened in Autumn. He had brought me sausage and *Le plaisir du texte* by Roland Barthes and he told me about the failure with the lotto. His system was perfectly correct and he had known exactly what he ought to have filled in to win the prize, but there had been something which caused him to enter numbers that were just that bit different. The prize had indeed fallen to the series from his system, and he had cursed himself and that worm within him. He had chances aplenty but he was doomed to squander them. He was sick to the back teeth of his theme. He was tired.

One day in autumn, he rang the doorbell and came up the stairs, mumbling. I awaited him in the doorway with the intention of quickly making it clear that his visit wasn't convenient and that I was afraid to get out of my rhythm were I to interrupt my work now. He was only halfway up the stairs when he held something up of which I couldn't see what it was.

'Look, look,' he said, excited, 'it's so bizarre!'

Without greeting me, he walked past me and allowed the bag to slip from his shoulder. The astrologer rarely lost sight of the social niceties and he had such a wild look in his eyes that I decided to give him a hearing for a moment, at least. He opened his hand and showed me what he had held up just now. It was a lipstick.

'Look,' he said, and he turned over its holder so I could

read the gold-coloured sticker at the end of it.

'Fruity Sorbet,' I read out aloud.

'The thirty-three,' he said, indignantly.

This startled me. Not to put a wet blanket on his unexpected cheerfulness, I said that it was indeed striking. The last few weeks, he had been going on about thirty-three all the time. According to him, this number had played a part in his life from infancy. He could remember street numbers, dates, hours, car number-plates and districts, capture them under this number and connect them with important experiences in his life, no matter where he had been in the world and at whatever age.

I had only realised how important this was to him when he had to make a choice about whether to move into a new house or whether to abandon this. The house being offered to him was many times better than the house he was living in at the time and by the look of things this was an opportunity he ought to grasp with both hands. No one would have doubted for even a second, but the astrologer was in a panic. When I asked him what his objections were, he said that he didn't yet know what street number he would have at his new address. The way things looked at the moment it would be number thirteen and he had nothing going with thirteen. A week later, he had received the message that he had been allotted the third floor.

'It's thirty-three after all,' he had said triumphantly. 'I'll be living at 13c and the c actually stands for a 3.'

Then he had packed his things and moved into the accommodation.

He stood opposite me and still had his coat on. Beaming, he told me about a sleepless night in which he had stayed awake because things continued to haunt him inside his head and he just could not decide whether he would stay on longer in the Netherlands or whether he would leave for France again. Only at daybreak had he slipped into a light slumber and he believed that he had decided to leave the Netherlands. Very sure of this he hadn't been at all. In the morning he had got up and had searched in his store cupboard for something to eat because – this had never happened before – he didn't feel like ordinary bread. What he did feel like, he didn't know. While pushing aside some tins and packages, he had suddenly seen a king-size thirty-three. It was the brand name of biscuits he had once brought from France and had left untouched ever since. This find strengthened him in the conviction of having made a good choice. He must leave the Netherlands as fast as possible.

The biscuits were stale but he had polished them off with relish. All of them. 'To get the thirty-three inside me, too,' he said.

Nothing could go wrong any more. He had begun to pack his suitcase and had decided to drop round at my place to say goodbye. On the threshold to my front door, he had knocked something with his foot that rolled away ahead of him and he had picked up this lipstick, on the back of which shone the magic number.

He looked at me as if he had won a great victory. Around his eyes there was a dark shadow and his eyelids were swollen and red, but every part of the eye that can glitter, did so, and I did not dare tell him what I thought.

He left that very same day. In the course of the evening I became nauseous and was sick. I thought I would never see him again.

And so it was, too.

You must tackle a talent the way you tackle life, for one day they will coincide, and your life will mean your talent and it will be your talent to live. A talent that remains a treacherous promise will be the death of you, of this I am convinced. It starts to rail cantankerously inside you about how life might have been and, at a certain moment, about how life ought to have been. That which ought to have drawn you up toward the beauty of a life of your own, toward its extraordinariness, in time pulls you down, towards death, the great equaliser.

When the astrologer had stood opposite me like that, warped with smouldering suffering, with that lipstick in his hand, it had suddenly got through to me to what extent we resembled one another and what distinguished us, the one from the other. What we did always boiled down to the same thing, but we felt ourselves to be subject to a different causality.

He left it to life outside him to convince him that his life had meaning, that it was rightfully his, that he had been incorporated into it, was doing well and that his life added up. Each day, he expected a pat on the back from the world, a sign from coincidence so that coincidence itself might be unmasked as a law and would change from a blind, indolent goddess into a soft, woeful mother who kept an eye on her offspring and guarded them continually. The astrologer could not bear the indifference of fate and because of this he could not bear life. He did not coincide with it.

Life had to free him from his horrible isolation by incorporating him in a big story and thus prove to him the necessity of his existence.

In my case, things were exactly the other way round. Isolation was the only position from which I believed I was able to free life of its meaninglessness, and from which I could turn the lonely, soulless things into signs, so that somewhere, in a context dreamed up by myself, they could have meaning.

Life needed me. Without me it didn't stand a chance.

Chapter II

THE EPILEPTIC

The philosophy lectures were given in two old buildings in
the centre of the city. These were the only buildings that
could measure up to the stately university buildings in
Oxford or Cambridge, the way I had seen them in films
and which to me had become the exemplars of what a
university is meant to look like. Though my student life in
no way matched the life of the heroes in such films, the
moment I passed between the columns flanking the
gateway and was borne along on the silence of the small,
circular green, I did have the idea of walking into a film
and of being involved in something distinguished.

At the centre of the little green stood a tall tree and on
the ground, in the shade of the leaves, there was a bust of
Minerva, placed on a plinth. When you walked in a curve
around her it was as if she followed you with her eyes and
this was why I would always avert my gaze and then would
be forced to behold the ugly stonework with the heads of
Vossius and Barleus carved out in it. I thought their heads
failures, but just the names of those two famous melancholiacs alone were sufficient to sustain momentarily the
atmosphere of being the elect, and for me to count myself
lucky to have ended up in a city of poets and men of
science. Any delusion of being special was wiped out the

moment I pushed open the glass doors and entered the building's large lobby. Here, the democratic spirit of the twentieth century reigned.

Public buildings may be able to retain history on the outside, but when they continue in use, the interior will assume the colour of the present. This is, strangely enough, because of the exterior of things and people, because of their shapes, their dress, the sound they make and because of their gestures. People follow fashions and whether in all those centuries the essence of man has changed, I prefer not to say. In any case, each century in its turn manages cunningly to nestle in the folds of people's clothes, in the choreography of their gestures, in the colour and tone of their words and in the drama of their emotions. Entire decades have withdrawn from the anonymity of time by hiding its progress behind the mask of their own, individual face, and the centuries always find people once again prepared to wear the mask of the age and thus to take charge of its character themselves.

In the lobby, there were groups of people everywhere and all kinds of bags in every colour and shape were lying scattered all over the place. Whenever I enter a place where so many people are standing together, I have the idea that I must know properly in advance what to do, then step up firmly to someone and get on with my business directly. To halt and think this over on the spot is impossible.

In the first instance, I had not detected anyone familiar and I went straight to the lift in one of the corridors that opened out on to the lobby. Next to the door to the lift there was a board with a plan of the building. I looked for the number of the large lecture theatre, H 211. It was in this theatre that Professor De Waeterlinck would be giving his formal lectures on contemporary philosophy.

'De Waeterlinck is a legend,' Daniel Daalmeyer had said to me, and his tales about the professor and the contents of his lectures had made me curious. He was the only philosophy teacher I had ever heard anyone speak of with admiration, up till now. The Netherlands are known for a painful lack of original philosophers and the lectures I had followed until then had given me every reason to subscribe to that judgement. As for the masters, I had only become acquainted with overgrown schoolkids with a command over the oeuvre of a foreign philosopher right down to the footnotes, and who particularly shone in retelling in other words that which had been put to paper in much finer prose by the philosopher himself. There was not one with his own tale to tell. It seemed as if there was a ban on coming out with an idea of your own. Abiding by the adage of student-participation, the greater part of the lectures had been turned into tutorials which boiled down to your having to defend ideas you didn't have in front of other students who didn't have any either. Mostly, there would be one or other megalomaniac twenty-year-old among a group of students like that, who believed himself an original thinker and who, during every tutorial, would grasp the opportunity to present at great length a discourse on his world view, or who wished to show how, at twelve years of age, he had already declared Kant's categoric imperative to be invalid.

What was encouraged by the lecturers was sheer torture to me and the reason why I avoided the tutorials as much as possible. I tried to arrange my studies in such a way that I was able to read books at home and follow the formal lectures in silence.

As with the interiors of the buildings, the lectures did not conform to the archetype of a university I held, either. The only things I liked from the very first day were the books.

34

I first saw Daniel Daalmeyer in 1981, during a course on Thomas Mann's *Der Zauberberg*, a collaborative project between literary science and philosophy. In the syllabus there was mention of 'a communal attempt to lay bare the roots of contemporary nihilism and the hard aesthetics of contemporary authors and philosophers'. In this one sentence there were so many things I knew nothing about that I decided to follow the course.

Every Tuesday afternoon an aspect of the novel would be addressed – by different people each time – and during one of those lectures I ended up next to a dark-haired boy to whom I paid no attention up to the moment he asked to borrow a pen from me.

I have only beautiful pens.

I don't like to lend my pens to anyone.

I can only lie when I have prepared myself for it days in advance.

The question about the pen came unexpectedly and I always have more than one in my bag. This the boy could not know, so it would have been easy to shake my head and if necessary to look at my neighbour apologetically, but I was bending down already and taking out the leather pen-case in which sat my beautiful *Lamy*. With an expression through which I actually did want to show something of the gravity of my gesture, I handed him the pen. He took it from my hands without deigning to look at either me or the pen, muttered 'Thanks' and began to write furiously in a small notebook. In the large lecture theatres the chairs were arranged as in an amphitheatre. The left arm-rest of each chair was provided with an extendable writing surface. He was left handed. His elbow almost reached the edge of my own writing surface and when the lecture started in a minute it would be impossible for me to get pen to paper myself because there was insufficient space for my right elbow.

I could see great difficulties ahead, became nervous, and prepared myself for the task, the moment the lecture started, of having to demand space for myself. In truth, I wanted my pen back this instant, best of all.

Meanwhile, a man of about forty was standing behind the lectern. Neatly suited, he took a folder from an expensive, leather briefcase. While occupied with this he looked markedly frequently in my direction, but when I followed his gaze, I noticed that his eyes were not directed at me but at the boy next to me. From the moment the latter had taken over my pen, he had not raised his head from the page again and I began to wonder what all those sentences on those little sheets of paper were about. To avoid contact with that elbow moving to and fro, I sat bolt upright and kept my stomach in. I wished that the man would set out on his lecture so that I could take to action. But he waited until the latecomers, too, had found a place in the lecture theatre and meanwhile he continued to watch the top of my neighbour's head.

This was the third lecture in the series and had as its subject the relationship between Hans Castorp and Clawdia Chauchat. I could not properly remember the name of the one who would be speaking today; I'd seen something like Muden or Uden down on the programme. What I was able to remember was the shopping list of publications mentioned underneath his name and the relatively young age at which his doctorate had been conferred.

My neighbour's elbow was still going to and fro. I was relieved when I heard the man behind the lectern ask a student to close the door behind him. I tapped on the writer's shoulder and, with the palms of my hand turned outward and a stupid expression on my face, indicated the precariousness of my position. He looked at me, dazed, as if I had drawn him out of a deep trance, looked at the tip of his own elbow, then at my writing surface, and said, far too loudly: 'Oh, I'm sorry.' A few people in front of us turned round. In a manner I knew from church, a blush rushed at me and I had the urge to begin to giggle and nod to everyone who felt annoyed. Nothing is so conducive to laughter as a situation in which it is forbidden to talk, to laugh or to utter any other sound at all. It cost me an effort to suppress my laughter. The boy next to me was little bothered by this and tried to turn his chair such that there would be sufficient space for me, too, to be able to write. If I pressed my right arm against my ribs, I could manage, and we nodded to one another to confirm the accommodation. He bent over his paper again and I looked at the speaker who meanwhile had introduced himself as being Stefan Duden and was elucidating the subject of the lecture.

What it is exactly, I don't know, nor do I know where such an attitude comes from, but the moment someone opens his mouth in order to speak, I don't want to miss a word of what is being said, even if the subject is of no importance whatsoever. I cling to the words of the presentation, lose awareness of my surroundings and feel myself to be on a journey. While I most definitely hear what the other is saying, at the same time I become introverted and something takes off in my head, a tumbling and tripping over of words, an interlinking of themes and images, evoked by random words of the other and set on track by these, a track on which I could not have set them myself. Somebody might be speaking about the connecting of a telephone to a network of cables and in so doing precisely use the particular words through which something about the nature of family life suddenly becomes clear to me, to give but an example.

There is something deceitful about it, for often it has happened that someone to whom I was speaking positively blossomed forth because I, through questions and comments, continuously encouraged the other by all means to go on telling more. Then I would realise that the teller would have to think that my enthusiasm stemmed from pure interest for the content of the tale as told, but it was especially the tale shaping in my head in parallel which excited me and which I wished to bring to a well-rounded whole.

As Duden's lecture progressed, the boy next to me was becoming ever more restless. At times he would mumble something, each time so loudly that the people in the row in front of us would look round, annoyed. His were disapproving remarks, at the delivery of which he would fiercely shake his head.

Though it irritated me, I was also curious as to what it was that was going on between Stefan Duden and the boy. I didn't doubt they knew each other even though the primer, since he had begun the lecture, had not looked in our direction again. The boy, on the contrary, now looked continuously in the speaker's direction and with clicking noises of his tongue he tried to attract Duden's attention.

Some ten minutes before the lecture was due to be interrupted for the interval, I heard my neighbour suddenly say 'No, no and again no!', saw how he edged his way out of his chair, stuffed the notepad and the pen into his coat pockets with a rough gesture and paved a way out for himself via the row in front of us. Without looking at Duden he said:

'For heaven's sake, man, give over. I know what you're really on about, Stefan.' He pronounced the name in a manner which gave rise to the suspicion that he knew more about him and wished to make it clear to everyone that in fact Stefan was called something else.

'There goes my pen,' coursed through me when the boy banged the lecture-theatre door shut behind him loudly.

Duden had watched him go, had turned his face toward the audience again and with a smile suggested beginning the interval a little early.

'In, let's say, a quarter of an hour I'll expect you all back here,' he had said. He remained standing behind the lectern and bent his head over his papers.

Outside, I looked around to see whether I could still see the boy anywhere, but the corridor was empty.

After the interval, the seat next to me remained unoccupied, but when I walked home via the Oudezijds Voorburgwal, I saw him come out of one of the side alleys. He was walking some ten metres ahead of me, staring at the ground, with his hands in his pockets. I quickened my step for now I would have a chance yet of demanding my pen back.

Whether his foot caught on a protruding clinker, I could not see, but I saw him trip suddenly and grab a low, cast-iron fence with his right hand. He did find some support but his left leg crumpled in slow motion and with an odd kind of curtsey he ended up on the ground. He stayed sitting there, his head bent. He looked devout.

I walked up to him quickly and tapped his shoulder. With a languid movement of his head he turned his face towards me. He was deathly pale and drops of sweat glistened pearl-like on his forehead and above his lip.

'Can I help you? Are you in pain?' I asked.

'I don't know yet. I'll stay like this for a while – wait.'

I hesitated, uncertain whether I, too, would kneel or would continue to stand upright beside him. With dwarves and lilliputians you have the tendency to make yourself as small as they are, to bend forward when you speak to them and that way bring your face down to their eye-level. You must suppress this tendency, for dwarves and lilliputians find this annoying and demeaning. Something like this was what shot through my head before I decided that I was in a

39

different situation, after all. I sat down on my heels beside him.

'Have you hurt yourself?' I asked.

He shook his head. His hand was still resting on the fence and I now saw that it had ended up directly on a protruding spike. He raised his head, saw what I was looking at, and sniggered. As if this had been quite enough for now, he stretched his back, drew breath with a sigh and took his hand away from the iron spike.

'Well, well, well,' he said and showed me the palm of his hand. In the centre there was a red dot but the skin was still intact.

'Splendid,' he said, 'perfectly splendid. A veritable stigma. It's truly too symbolic for words.'

He laughed, mockingly, and I laughed along with him. I like people who are sensitive to symbols and I had the notion that his laugh about the 'stigma' had something to do with his behaviour towards Stefan Duden. I supported him in getting up and I was just about to remind him that he had gone off with my pen when he slapped me on the shoulder and said:

'Theresa, comforter of the sick, you deserve a drink.'

That's how I ended up that afternoon in a little café in the Hoogstraat, where the boy introduced himself.

'Daniel Daalmeyer, epileptic. Thirty-two, an epileptic for nine years, of which the first seven years extremely actively so, and currently an epileptic-retired.'

He told me he was never sure whether he tripped over something or had a moment of 'absentia' and in order to avert a fit would sink to his knees in advance to head off falling. It was all a waste of time, really. The medication had improved continually and real attacks like the ones he used to have had failed to appear for two years now. He had the idea that although his head, over the years, had taken to suppressing the falling-about, his body refused to

40

trust blindly in the effect of the pills. It clung to an old habit and lagged behind his brains. His legs in particular showed themselves to be hard of learning and suspicious. They understood little of his moods and to them the least imaginable emotion was the herald of a fall. All fear and excitement were swept into a single pile by his legs and were understood to be the signal to weaken and relax.

At the start of the conversation, he had given an impression of being tired but during the telling Daniel's eyes gained more and more sheen. His voice became brighter and most noticeably louder.

He spoke of his illness as if it were a self-willed creature which had joined him one fine day, never to leave again. He had come to love it, in his own way. Because of the creature, he had become someone he himself could watch with amazement and about whom he was curious because his own behaviour had become unpredictable to himself. There were moments when he discovered himself in rooms unknown to him, surrounded by caring people he had never met in his life before. Events happened to him, but the great organiser of what happened to him was not external to him, but within himself. He loved that creature more unconditionally than he had ever loved anyone before. He was happy, without a grain of envy, to allow it the pleasure of mocking him, to deceive his nerves and to muck about with his muscles. Inside, it carefully staged hilarious tableaux, though the medicines had made sure that these were no longer anything more than contests in false moves.

'It's a vicious little imp and at times I imagine how she sits on the edge of my pituitary and, roaring with laughter, slaps her thighs. She's had more fun with me than anyone else has ever had, let me tell you. It's been less so the last few years, of course, and there's not so much fun to be had with me any more. It's odd, but I regret that at times. The

41

medicines are a blessing yet at the same time they have destroyed something for me, something between that imp and me. At times I'm afraid she has disappeared altogether and that the medicines have done for her, but on a day like today I know she still lives and her sense of humour hasn't lost any of its originality. I've fallen in love with the illness,' he roared with laughter, adding 'three cheers for the illness!' and he ordered another glass of beer for himself and a red wine for me.

It happens more often that I meet somebody for the first time and then ask myself whether I could fall in love with that man. Once I do this, there's no point in bothering, for I won't. Daniel Daalmeyer was handsome in a way which I only learned to see through the eyes of other women. The way another can learn to appreciate modern Art, African fertility statues or poetry in the course of his life, thus I had had to learn to see the beauty of men. I myself did not have an eye for it.

From the day I attended schools where the classes consisted of both girls and boys, my girl friends had had to point out to me that someone was in love with me. I hadn't a clue because I hardly spent any attention on the boys in class. In the main, I was in love with the schoolmaster. Masters were rarely handsome but they knew a lot and had read books. Because these loves were covert and I kept them from my friends, I could never make it clear to them why I, in my turn, did not fall in love with the boys who were in love with me. But he had such beautiful eyes, they said, such sweet curls, such a roguish laugh. Then I would see that the boy indeed possessed all that was described to me by the girls, but in my eyes he did not really improve. He had the one failing because of which he just could not become desirable to me: he was young.

Daniel had dark-blond, straight hair. It would slip forwards each time he moved his head. There was a parting in the middle and when the hair fell like a curtain in front of his eyes he would pull back with his hand the two, heavy locks that fanned out, where they would then rest on his skull a moment, subsequently to drop forward again. His face was narrow with very regular features. Two prominent cheekbones and the slightly almond-shaped eyes gave him an Indian appearance, something a flawless, golden yellow complexion did its best to enhance. Daniel Daalmeyer was handsome, very handsome even, but Daniel Daalmeyer was young.

'Young' is not a word that applies to years, for Daniel was older than I. 'Young' is a judgement.

'Go on,' I said to Daniel when he returned with the drinks. The story of his illness had enchanted me and his image of the imp had set me thinking. Meanwhile I was again busy getting clarity on something I so needed to become clear to me it seemed.

He'd had his first attack at twenty-four. He was studying medicine, attended an evening course in painting at the Rietveld Academy, was a member of a drama group and was unhappy. He felt he could become anything he wanted to and wasn't able to choose just one of the possibilities. GP, surgeon, psychiatrist, artist, actor, director, no matter what he hurled himself into, it seemed to him that he would be able to attain great heights in any field if only he were able to choose. Cutting up flesh, painting and acting came to him with equal ease and this was why he had been imbued with a feeling of futility for he already knew that which he was studying to be. His life resembled a pot of magnificent shards in which he could only recognise fragments of himself and never the complete person. He had but one desire left: to become whole, to gather himself up and meet at a single point.

'And then *she* came.'

Epilepsy had been his saviour; ever since he'd had her, his life revolved around her. She made him a man in one piece. She bunched up that which until then had lain before him as a possibility: medicine and art. Now, he was only interested in philosophers and writers who had something to report about this illness, and read auto-biographies and biographies of everyone who had suffered from it-did-not-matter-which abnormality. He scoured medical encyclopaedias from beginning to end and especially enjoyed the theories concerning his own disease without neglecting those concerning other ones, either. As an epileptic, he himself had become the focal point of his own life and his principal object of study.

'Aren't you sickening for something nice, Theresa?' he asked, suddenly. 'That would really win me over tremendously.'

I blushed. Why? Did I want to win him over? Was it strange to be addressed by him as 'Theresa' when I had introduced myself to him quite clearly? Or did the question take me by surprise, did it disturb my joy in listening too much and, moreover, did it cross my intention to ask him as soon as possible about his relations with the man who had given a lecture about *Der Zauber-berg* this afternoon?

It might be, too, that I had nothing with which to compete with the poetry of epilepsy. Every other illness looked paltry by comparison; I was fit as a fiddle. I had been getting treatment from a skin specialist since I was eighteen, it was true, but I had never experienced my skin troubles as being an illness: a nuisance, at most.

'No,' I replied, 'I'm not sickening though my wrappings are indeed a little icky.'

'Wonderful!' Daniel cried, loudly, 'mange, eczema, psoriasis, acne, boils, sores, warts, haemorrhoids, itching, peeling, the diseases of the skin, the faults in the surface of the tissue, tremendously interesting. I'm serious,' he added when I looked at him, surprised.

'The ailments of the skin are quintessentially the mark of ambivalent individualists, what am I saying, *hyper*-individualists. There's enough to be said about it and as regards mystery they're no way inferior to mine, though you've been a little more stingily provided for by the philosophers. Even so, metaphors, myths and speculations a-plenty. I got myself into a terrible rage about our dear Susan Sontag. There she goes, wading into battle with the metaphors of disease, no less, as if things aren't bad enough. The only thing that makes having a disease worthwhile is the crystallisation of yourself into a much-encompassing metaphor. Only through metaphor is every possible kind of experience to be gleaned from the illness and only through metaphor do you end up with folk whom otherwise you'd have failed to run into, with angels or devils, accordingly.'

'And to which category do I belong?'

'Look, in a certain way you and I, by the logic of our diseases, stand diametrically opposed to one another. The hidden, dark mechanism of the brain opposite the brutal, exhibitionistic visibility of the skin. We, the epileptic ones, are delivered into the hands of the mercy of our environment. In essence it should leave us cold what others think of us, for we will turn ourselves inside out shamelessly if necessary. If you occupy yourself too much with the way others see you, your writhing body with that distorted mug, your foaming mouth and your rolling eyes, then you had better choose a different disease, for you'd have no life with epilepsy in that case. You fall down and you rely on it that there will always be people again who catch you or scrape you up from the ground, that's what it boils down to.

'And that's the strange thing, for appearances are

45

against us, every disease has appearances against it. What seems a mysterious disease at first is in fact a disease with an unabashed, bombastic public display. Epilepsy, despite yourself, shamelessly exposes your innermost self to the eye of the outside world. There is no way to conceal anything. So, directly opposite this theatrical disease with its invisible source are the diseases of the skin, of the exterior appearance therefore. If I'm allowed to maintain the metaphor of the theatre a moment, then someone with a skin disease is always going about on full view. If your face is covered in boils, this is an ineradicable make-up. Disease of the exterior appearance divulges itself instantly, there is little obscuring to be done. And yet this open erosion of the armour is known as the disease of exceptionally introverted, suspicious people. It's a great mistake to think that afflictions of the skin come about because of such a thing as a thin, over-sensitive skin which the dirt of the world is able to penetrate too easily, and that the sufferer falls short in his resistance to the damaging influences from outside. Again, the opposite is true here, too, Theresa. Skin diseases come about especially in people who actually arm themselves against the world and wish to foster so much hard skin on their soul that no one will ever truly be able to penetrate, reaching down to them. People with a skin disease do not reject their dead cells, they systematically build towards an elephant-skin and it's just such a thick skin which is a luxuriant breeding place for growths, inflammations, itches, boils and pimples. The skin is so thick it chokes that lot inside and blocks the way to everything that needs space and air. In short, that which seems a perfectly visible, exterior, unhidden disease, is precisely the disease of the one who hides. You're such a one, too, a veiled woman. Am I right, or am I right?'

I was too bowled over by this interpretation of disease to be able to think whether it was right or not. The word 'veil'

46

could send me into rapture and I was almost pleased with afflictions to which there was so much to be analysed. Where had all this been written down? How did one get hold of this kind of knowledge? I asked Daniel: titles, authors, professors whose lectures in medicine I could begin to attend.

'The book in which all this is written does not yet exist,' Daniel replied, 'it is the result of my life as an epileptic. The only one able to write it am I, I fear. The paradox of the sufferer has become clear to me from all those case histories I devoured so voraciously. The sufferer turns out to be floored each time by something he precisely needed to protect his most vulnerable spot. Hegel's scheme of life is the blueprint to the biography of the sufferer.'

Our glasses were empty again and it was getting busier in the boozer. I asked Daniel whether he wanted one for the road and, leaning against the edge of the bar, I recovered from the tale and his uninterrupted stream of words. It looked like Daniel could go on like this for hours yet. He himself relished his own explanations no less than I did and at times I was under the impression that he was discovering fresh connections on the spot and, enthusiastic about his own discoveries, believed himself to be ever closer to the truth of the subject that occupied him most: Daniel Daalmeyer himself.

I returned to the table with the wine and the beer. He suddenly looked washed out and afterwards the conversation never really took off again. He had jumped the tracks of his own tale and could no longer retrieve the rhythm by which he had been able to recount so compellingly. We exchanged a few things about how long we had been studying, what else we had occupying us, our addresses. He turned out to be living not that far away from me and he invited me to come over for dinner that weekend. I took out my diary and suddenly thought of my pen.

'You must still have my pen somewhere,' I said and was a bit ashamed of myself. I was reminded again of events in the lecture theatre, of his incomprehensible behaviour toward Stefan Duden. I had let the moment pass to ask about that.

It was a quarter to seven. I had estimated the walk from my home to Daniel Daalmeyer's house to take a quarter of an hour. Via the Haarlemmerdijk I could cut through to Bickerseiland and look at leisure for the warehouse Daniel had mentioned.

At that stage, I didn't yet know that as a woman it was best to arrive between ten minutes and half an hour late for an appointment with a man. I would always be dead on time.

I wondered what his home would look like and what kind of meal he would have prepared. Things like that do say something about somebody.

Number 162 was a large building. The windows had shutters of which the dark green paint was peeling off here and there. Judging by the number of doorbells, more than ten people lived in the house. I looked for Daniel's name. While my eyes cursorily took in the names one by one, they suddenly halted at a name I knew: Duden.

'That's why,' I thought, though I didn't know what causality was involved. Reading the name evoked a strange kind of tension, the tension I had also felt in the lecture theatre and one I could not explain.

Underneath Duden it said 'DD', without full stops. Because these might just as easily be someone else's initials, I looked on down the list but I didn't see 'Daniel Daalmeyer' in full anywhere, and so I rang at 'DD'. Meanwhile I took the bottle of wine from my bag. When the door wasn't opened immediately I had to suppress a fearful presentiment. Perhaps I hadn't pressed the bell button firmly enough. I tried again and pressed my thumb down quite hard on the white button. At the same time I listened intently whether I could hear the bell, but this wasn't the case. By taking a few steps back I could look up along the front gable and oversee the windows, but there was no movement to be seen behind the open shutters and the closed ones stayed that way.

With a queer feeling in my stomach I pressed the bell another time, already despondent and with the intention of leaving in a moment, for I felt myself to be watched by all kinds of invisible eyes. I put the bottle back into my bag, ready, so as to look a little less ridiculous.

Had he forgotten our appointment? Had I made a mistake and did we have an appointment for the following Sunday? Had something happened because of which he was suddenly indisposed and had my name slipped his mind so the telephone book was of no use to him and he hadn't been able to reach me?

What I hadn't wanted to think of but which was precisely what I now began to imagine, was how Daniel was lying there writhing on the floor of his house, foam on his lips, the door locked and no one at hand to help him.

I simply cannot stand it when things don't go the way I had thought them to previously.

It is just like going downstairs and misjudging the number of steps. You think there is still one more to come and this thought likewise occupies the muscles of your legs. And then you're down already. Your foot comes down with a bang in the same place, a violent marching-on-the-spot which that same moment renders all the muscles' effort perfectly useless and ridiculous. That's the way it feels, too. It makes me furious, a thing like that.

Having looked up a further time, I turned round and wanted to return the way I had come when I heard someone call out 'Hello?'. From one of the opened windows protruded the head of the man who had given the lecture.

'I've come to see Daniel Daalmeyer,' I cried. 'We have an appointment but he's not there.'

'Just a sec,' he said and his head disappeared from the frame.

A moment later the door was being opened. I entered a broad, dark hallway. 'Two stairs up,' he cried and I was just searching by touch for the first step up when someone upstairs switched on the hallway light. At the top of the second flight of stairs Duden was standing waiting for me. He put out his hand.

'Hello, I'm Stefan – pleased to meet you. My wife is taking a look upstairs to see if Daniel is perhaps home after all. Meanwhile, do come in, if you like.'

I felt at a loss and I also don't like it when strangers go out of their way on my behalf, but above all I am curious and I stepped past him on to the landing of his dwelling. There I waited until he had closed the front door behind him and went ahead of me to the sitting room.

The sitting room was as large as a ballroom and designed to provoke cries of admiration. These I, too, brought forth. It looked almost a museum, full of Jugendstil stuff. The floor was made of unvarnished wooden boards, along two walls there were bookcases and no matter where I looked the frilly Jugendstil motifs would turn up. Furniture, tables, mirrors, lamps, statuettes on marble columns, drawings on the walls.

'Nice house,' I said, 'most aesthetic.'

'Yes, we're very pleased with it, too.'

The situation was not one in which to go and take a look at everything at length. I tried to discover as much as possible from the settee where I had taken a seat. He asked whether I would like something to drink and I said that I didn't want to be a bother to him.

'We rather like unexpected visitors,' he reassured me, 'and Daniel's friends know that they're always welcome here, too.' Then he put me at my ease and listed the drinks from which I could make my choice. Campari. He walked over to a walnut cabinet with some of those inlay-motifs. 'I'll just go and fetch some ice from the kitchen,' he said and he walked into the hallway with two filled glasses. I heard the front door open and close and then I heard a woman's voice. There was talking in hushed tones. I could not hear what they were saying to one another. This I thought a pity.

Even before Duden returned with the drinks, a slim woman whirled into the room, walked with steady tread in my direction and ordered me even from a distance not to trouble myself to get up. She shook my hand firmly, gave her name as being Lisa and said that strangely enough she'd had no reply at Daniel's.

'Not at all like DD,' she said and she tried to hide by talking how sharply she was observing me.

'On the rare occasion he does make an appointment, he would never forget, so I don't know what's up either. Have you known each other long?'

Going into too much of a rigmarole, I explained to her that I had known Daniel for but a short while and I hinted at the fact that we both were at the same school and had nothing else to bother our fair heads over than philosophy and other airy-fairy stuff.

For some reason or other I had the feeling I had to set her mind at rest.

I don't think I get on well with other women. They make me insecure and when I feel insecure I only say things which I believe someone else dearly wants to hear. I myself don't think any more then. Conversely, I am also under the impression that women want to comfort me and they in their turn say things which they think that *I* dearly wish to

51

hear. This particular way gets you nowhere, of course.

Since the woman had come in, I felt ill at ease, lured into a trap. I no longer wondered where Daniel would be and why our appointment had gone awry but I did wonder how he would react to my visiting Duden and his wife. I had the idea that he would find it annoying.

'Why, Mr Duden, are you so interested . . .' I began in the end.

'Stefan,' interrupted Stefan Duden.

'Oh, yes, yes of course ... Stefan, why are you so interested in that Thomas Mann?'

'How d'you mean: *that* Thomas Mann.' he said and he looked at me with a friendly smile. 'Don't you like *that* Thomas Mann?'

'Frankly: no,' I said and realised meanwhile that it would not cost me any effort at all to address him as 'Stefan'. He was a master, it was true, but one without authority. He was too young and there was something about him, something proper and studied, something through which he had always continued to be a student. It provoked in me the urge, at last, to give him a big, fat 'Fail', for once.

'I find him so wordy and long-winded. The novels bore me and the things in his essays you can find in those of others, and better to boot. I think he's a pedant, too. He only wants to show that he's read a lot of books, according to me, and that he's also capable of doing something himself with all those philosophies and theories. They're not good novels, in my opinion.'

'Yes,' he said, 'this complaint is often heard about Thomas Mann. But what makes his books unreadable to one is to another precisely their most attractive quality. I myself very much love the intertwining of philosophy and literature and the mixing of different kinds of text. Mann does show how an intellectual, during a very curious period of our century, handled the knowledge of those days. His novels are a repository of thought in the early twentieth century and they are also imbued with a specific complex of questions concerning identity which stems from a number of historical givens. Of course, Mann himself, as an individual, wrestled tremendously with the problem of his own identity, too, but according to me he has succeeded in raising the personal to a higher plain and elevated his own problems of identity to that of world literature.'

While Duden was speaking, Lisa had walked from the room. This worried me and I was afraid of having tackled things badly. When dealing with a couple you must divide your attention equally. Before you know, you're hanging on to every word of the most fluent speaker and the third party feels excluded or not taken seriously.

I resolved to ask Lisa about her activities in a moment. I was, moreover, curious about them, but you can't do everything at once, after all.

'Ah well: the problem of identity interests me, also in the way it is treated by other authors, for that matter. The thing I find so clever with Mann, is how he has connected this theme with his three principal ones: illness, death and being an artist.'

Lisa returned from the kitchen and set down a bowl of olives on the table.

'That's the strange thing, you know, with that Mann fellow,' I said, 'I find everything others say about him much more exciting than his own novels. That's the way it goes with me during this course at school, too. Time and again, I hear something which makes me think that I really must finally finish reading *Der Zauberberg* in its entirety because apparently there are all kinds of things in it that have my concern too. But when I read the novel itself once more, I can't find them. After some ten pages or so, I think

53

the better of it once again. I just can't get through it. Are you in literature too?' I asked, following on immediately while turning to Lisa.

'No,' she said and she smiled, 'though it does seem like that at times – no, I do something different.'

She did not say what in fact this was.

So I asked.

A psychiatrist.

Has anyone ever understood, truly understood, why people blush? Who? Perhaps people become psychiatrists because they are addicted to the manic fear they bring about in somebody when they say what they do.

You sometimes hear of people who have had a very serious accident and who, just before they thought they would die, saw their entire life pass before them in a flash. Something similar happened to me now, only I didn't have my entire life in view but that short while from the moment she had entered the room. How had I been behaving? What might be gleaned from this? What did she think of my gnawed-down nails? Had my hand felt clammy when we introduced ourselves? Was I laughing too much or too little? Did she understand why I blushed?

Just as the blushing threatened to become so severe that I thought I would have to excuse myself, there was a rap on the door.

'There's the prodigal,' Stefan said and he got up. Lisa was quicker and was already walking toward the door.

'Have you seen little Theresa,' I heard Daniel ask in a loud, laughing voice. Lisa spoke a good deal more quietly. I could not hear what she said. I bent down to pick up my bag from the floor, got up, thanked Stefan for the kind reception I'd had, and walked into the hallway. He walked after me. Daniel was standing in the doorway and interrupted Lisa mid-sentence in order to greet me.

'Are you coming?' he asked and hoisted a plastic carrier

54

into the air. 'Dinner for two.'

'Thanks again,' I said and I shook Lisa's hand. She looked at me, her face motionless, which made me feel uneasy and at the same time made me think that she had something mysterious about her. Without paying any further attention to Lisa and Stefan, Daniel turned his back on them and walked in the direction of the broad staircase.

The more churlishly others behave, the more I have the feeling I must be extremely correct. I nodded amiably at the couple once more, said 'Thanks' again, and 'So nice to have met you,' and then I followed Daniel who had already climbed halfway up the stairs to the upper floor and was standing there, waiting.

'Was it really awful?' he asked as he walked on. I didn't know whether he meant the enforced wait or the short-lived stay with his friends, and failed to reply.

Before he swung open the door, he had already said that it would be rather a disappointment after the Duden's luxurious showroom.

Disappointment is not the right word. Disappointment belongs to screwed-up expectations and there is a difference between having expectations and plain curiosity.

Daniel, as I learned a moment later, lived in Lisa and Stefan's storage space. The enormous loft of the warehouse had been divided up with wooden partitions into several different storage spaces belonging to the apartments of the inhabitants. Lisa and Stefan, 'my benefactors', had ceded their loft space to Daniel and seen to it that he was also allowed to use the adjacent area of one of the neighbours. Out of the bare space they had made a habitable living room, comparable with a studio flat as regards surface area, like the ones many students had in the city.

He had explained it all rather hurriedly and sought to change the subject as quickly as possible rather than discuss his friendship with Lisa and Stefan Duden. So, if I was going to find out as much as I could about what bound these three people to one another, I would have to rely on tactics. When necessary, I can be very tenacious in such matters.

What happened to him regularly had of course happened to him again this time: he had forgotten to replenish his supply of pills before the weekend, discovered it half an hour before I was due and had cycled over quickly to his father's house. 'The doctor-poet', Daniel called him, a psychiatrist and at the same time one of the doctors in charge of his case.

'That's an unhealthy father-son relationship,' he said, 'you don't need to tell me. More than enough Freud's gone down the gullet here.'

For emergency rations he had a sure-fire address on one of the canals where his father had his practice and lived in the rest of the building. Since his father had begun to write poetry and had made a catch of a young girlfriend, he never left the house any more.

Once arrived there, he again had been forced to listen to it all: that his father suspected him of forgetting the pills on purpose, of wanting to be ill, and so forth, with the result that his already tight calculation on timing was doomed to fail, and that at a certain moment he knew for sure he would turn up too late for our appointment.

'Once I've realised something like that, I let things slip altogether.'

On the way back he had bought two pizzas. He had been convinced that we would not miss one another. 'I am surrounded by guardian angels.'

I told him that, as far as I was concerned, he might do

well next time not to count too much on their assistance. I think my mood dipped for a moment. I don't really like pizza that much.

There were few items of furniture in his room but those that were there were antiques. They'll be cast offs of his parents, I thought, and imagined what it must have been like to grow up as a child in posh rooms.

In the village where I was born, most people were quite simple folk, as were my parents. There were only a few prominent residents: the mayor, the doctor, the notary and some members of the aristocracy who lived in manor houses on the edge of the village. The children of these prominent citizens were different. They didn't run; they walked upright and bashed their knees in falls a lot less frequently. They had different toys as well. We had spinning tops, balls and elastic. They had a diabolo, walked with books on their heads and later they were given a horse.

Our kind of children played from the age of ten in the brass band; they were given piano lessons at home and on Sundays they would listen to *Peter and the Wolf*. There were differences: you could see that instantly. But ours was the majority and from belonging to the majority we derived our pride and strength.

Looking back, this strikes me as odd.

At university, all the prominent children of the country had come together and now they formed the majority. They had all walked about with books on their heads and they all knew *Peter and the Wolf* backwards. Theirs were tales about the decline of the aristocracy – some of these were quite hilarious. It's the way you tell 'em.

Someone like myself is what I should have looked for. This I did not do.

I preferred not to meet someone such as myself.

To belong to the minority gave me strength.

'Decline' was a word whose meaning I didn't understand. What was it we had that could fall into decline? Nothing but our bodies but this applied to them too, surely, for death knows of no exceptions. Death is for all. And this was not what the others meant when they were talking about decline.

Daniel was busy with the plates, the cutlery and the pizzas in the same way that I had seen him writing before Duden's lecture started. He disappeared completely into his activities, directed his eyes with a rigid gaze on to the things in his hands and seemed utterly to forget his surroundings. This was also the way he ate, staring at his plate with a slice of pizza in his hand.

I have many memories of eating and sometimes I remember having been pleased to have got it over with. This is what has stuck with me of that evening with Daniel, too.

Only once we were sitting opposite one another again, each slouched in a chair, a glass of wine in hand, did my irritation abate and I calmed down.

I looked at him and thought him handsome. It occurred to me that I wouldn't mind having a body like Daniel's: bony, tall, slim hips, broad shoulders and encased in a strong, smooth and tawny skin. Just now, when he walked up the stairs ahead of me, I had caught myself imitating the way he walked, the nonchalance of the manner in which he swung his legs out ahead of him and allowed his torso to undulate upon that springy step. He had been wearing a leather biker-jacket. On coming in he had carelessly tossed it over a chair.

I asked him whether I might just try it on.

Sure.

'It smells completely of boy,' I said to Daniel, because I

thought it embarrassing to stand in silence in front of the mirror to look at myself. I felt tough and inviolable and resolved to keep an eye out at once for exactly such a jacket. This resolve excited me.

Daniel had barely taken any notice of the dressing-up session. He was sitting on his heels in front of a stack of papers.

'I've done some research, Theresa,' he said.

I sat myself down in an armchair again. With a scholarly article in his hand, he came and sat on the arm of my chair and bent forward in order to read a number of passages together with me, passages he had marked in advance. It was about language, illness and thought. Somebody had done research into people with skin conditions and Daniel said that he was very curious as to whether I recognised myself in a certain description of character. He handed me the paper and as I read he leaned against me to read along with me.

I could barely concentrate on the quotations.

It was something about the idea of continually being plagued by the world, about unreal feelings of independence and individuality and the agony experienced when authority threatened ostensible individuality. Though the jargon palled upon me, the data did shake me. I would very much have liked to read the paper in peace, if only I'd felt more at ease, without the hurried nervousness with which I now let my eyes course over the print. A reader is defenceless.

I wanted Daniel off my armrest; I put the paper back on his chair and said that I thought it was going too far indeed to go and rummage through the soul just because of a pimple.

Instead of being offended, Daniel laughed and put a hand underneath my chin. He wanted to bring his face to mine. I didn't.

59

'No,' said I.

'Why not?'

'You don't give a fig for love, according to me,' I said.

'Who says I'm doing this for love?' he said.

This made me laugh.

'That's just it,' I said.

He laughed about that.

'Doctora mystica,' he said, and then for both of us all that was over and done with. I was glad that he hadn't spent hours in the kitchen in order to prepare a splendid meal for me and present me with one delicious dish after another, proudly served in tattered tureens, dressed with a touchingly clumsy garnish, and pudding for afters, too. I couldn't have stood that. Then it would have been more difficult to say 'no'.

That evening, I didn't find out much more about his friendship with Lisa and Stefan other than that at one time they had formed a fine *Dreigestirn*, as Daniel put it.

'She loves me because I am ill and he loves her most when she loves someone who is ill, and I haven't wondered for ages anymore whether I love someone so I let it all come over me. Commonplace story, love-triangle, all love is interceded for and demands a third party, cliché of desire, not worth pondering on.'

He wasn't willing to say any more about it.

He adopted this same curt tone when I asked him about his father. Grudgingly he told how he had been lumbered with an alliterating name by his father.

'And my sister's called Dana, so it's not hard to imagine what those poems start to look like. They're about emotions and moods of which we only saw in his poetry that he had them and which we didn't believe in. "Wouldn't you just love to experience what you experience in your poems," I would always think. He so dearly

60

wants to feel himself what those poor sods feel who come to him with their tales of total madness, with their overheated view of the world and the peculiar figments of their imagination. But that man doesn't even dare to go out on the street on his own, let alone does he have the courage to relinquish control and abandon himself to that cruddy load of muddle and mayhem inside his own head.'

He looked me in the face and said: 'Enough now about the doctor, Theresa. Ever been to a shrink? You'd doubtlessly be impressed by my father. Women fall for him. They think he's such an engaging, fascinating personality because he says so little and when he does say something it's about their own little soul. That's what women love so, don't they: silent men who all day have nothing else on their minds but the state of their female souls? True or not true?'

What do you, a woman, say to that?

'But perhaps you won't love him. You are too much alike. You too can listen so terribly passionately.'

With Daniel I would repeatedly feel my anger rise, anger which a moment later disappeared completely and then provoked a great feeling of relief. I did not know what to make of him. At times I thought him cut loose, a mocking, introverted child who loses himself in his game and with artless casualness expects the care and protection of the people around him. Other times I saw him as a desolate daemon who sees the world sharply, who with an almost animal intuition understands how it truly works and therefore without any scruples sets the people in his surroundings to work for him. Of course, afterwards he would secretly have to despise those who helped him, because he thought everyone stupid who did not see through his ruses.

61

Chapter III

THE PHILOSOPHER

The entrance to H 211 lay at the highest point. From there I looked down into the depths upon a half-moon shaped circle with chairs and unbroken rows of tables. I was in plenty of time but the hall was already more than half full of people. They were sitting with their backs towards me and I could look round at leisure to see whether I could recognise the back of Daniel Daalmeyer. I didn't know yet what I should do were I indeed to discover him, whether I would go up to him or avoid him. I was now wearing just such a biker jacket as he was and I was afraid of his mocking, doubtlessly shrewd interpretation of my purchase.

Ever more people were slipping past me through the doorway and by and by the hall was becoming full. I gave up the search for Daniel and walked to the nearest row in which nobody was sitting yet.

Taking a seat on one's own in a hall and being there in order to listen to a speaker is a pleasure I know from the past when I would frequently go to church on my own and slip into a pew. Everyone had gathered to be alone with the same thing. It's an event not to be compared with anything else. At one time I did expect the same thing from the theatre, but the theatre didn't take me in that way. I have never experienced it anywhere else again. In church and in class.

The lecture was to begin at a quarter past eleven but at twenty-five past eleven the platform was empty still. The hall remained remarkably quiet. There was a bit of a hubbub but this was dampened down by an expectant silence I had never yet heard at a formal lecture. You came here to listen, not for company or in order to meet others. The audience waited for the man of whom Daniel had said that he was a legend, a miracle of eloquence and erudition.

'He's not so much someone with his own philosophy but he is certainly capable of opening up new worlds to you in the space of two hours, to set you on a track, to acquaint you with more writers and books than you will be able to read ever in your life. He manages to lay connections between the most diverse matters and yet you have the idea all the while of being addressed in person about something you just happen to be occupied with.'

'What's so legendary about the philosopher?'

'De Waeterlinck is someone you simply have to turn into a legend. He's so elusive. How he manages it, I don't know, but he refuses to put a single word down on paper. Ever since he was appointed professor he's never published another word and it's said about him that he went all out to get back every printed copy of his thesis so he'd be able to destroy the lot. Apparently, he even loathes setting his own signature to something. He signs passnotes with an illegible, ever-changing scrawl, nothing more.'

De Waeterlinck walked on to the platform through a side door. A number of people in the hall applauded. He was a large man, solidly built, with a square head, all grey-haired. I don't know whether, from the moment Daniel told me about him, I had expected it, or whether the legend had done its work, but I saw it without being surprised: De Waeterlinck had the face.

It's a face other men bear, too, like a single face, always the same. I know it and I encounter it. It is the face of a public man and I, who belong to the public, wish to be designated by him. He must choose me above all others, lift me clear from among the others, make me special, abstract me from the masses I am among and with which, from the moment I saw him, I am no longer at peace. A Carmen syndrome. God knows how I got it.

He settled behind the table and cleared his throat. He welcomed us. It was then that I heard he spoke Flemish. I couldn't believe my ears.

'It is a pleasure to see that once more you have turned up in great numbers. But perhaps I ought not to say that. Should Nietzsche be right and pain, despair, melancholy and bitter misfortune are the *conditio sine qua non* for independent thought, then my pleasure is perhaps unseemly. Who knows, you might all, as you sit here, be deeply disillusioned; you might all have the paranoid feeling that everyone is setting traps for you, enticing you and then turning their backs on you, or perhaps you feel yourself to be perfectly ridiculous and you are taunted by terrible doubts as to your firmness of character; or you might be plotting revenge to punish others for their continual betrayal – these are all equally conceivable, are they not?

'If so, be comforted: you are in any case on the right track for, according to that same Nietzsche, you should not be spared any of this if you wish to practise the art of thought. Once you have mastered this art, he promises you the highest form of happiness, but do not take offence at me when I leave Nietzsche to account for that promise and do not make it to you personally.

'I promise you no happiness. I don't even promise to impart the art of thought to you. I wouldn't know how to go about that. I can't do much more than acquaint you with the men who did believe themselves capable of alleviating the existence of others. I consider their attempts as being of great nobility but their diversity and mutual differences are possibly more likely to give you the desperate feeling of having to roam a dark forest of philosophical ideas than to give you a taste of that promised happiness. I don't wish you to lose your way.

'As I just said, I cannot do more for you than to show you a little of the lie of the land in this forest. To find happiness, if you do still believe in this, you will have to set about it in other ways.'

There was muted laughter in the hall. Not mine. The feeling finally to have found something which I had been in search of fruitlessly for years, tended to make me a bit of a cry-baby and sentimental, if anything.

Can you seek something when you do not know what it is?

I sought without knowing what.

When I do find it, I recognise it without knowing what it is. I recognise it because it always comes in the same form, in the same casing, in the shape of words, of the speaking man with the face, or of the words on paper behind which this face hides, too. The man and the words evoke a desire I wish to slake and retain at the same time; which makes me suffer and which I relish; which I wish to fathom and want to keep a mystery; and of which I think, at times, that it coincides with life, and at other times that it coincides with the words and is no more than this, that without words it does not exist, is nothing any more.

Interval.

The listeners thronged out of the hall on their way to the canteen. I remained seated.

A number of people remained seated, too, on the front row: elderly people, I now saw. De Waeterlinck had clambered down from the platform via the steps and he shook hands with the older people, one by one. He spoke with them, listened, laughed amiably. He was accessible.

I watched. I was happy. Today something had started that would last, that was special and one-off, and of which, while it was still happening, I was already thinking in retrospect.

Two elderly men had got up and were standing, busily gesticulating, next to the philosopher. The one man was small, slight and tawny, had a balding head and a face with sharply drawn features. He was soberly dressed but with meticulous care. The other was a little larger, sturdier and somewhat portly. His hair was long and grey, curling down into his neck and he had a colourful cravat tied round his neck. Beneath a baggy, ill-fitting jacket shimmered the bright red of a jersey or cardigan. Both men were wearing glasses.

By the way in which they were standing, leaning now on the one then on the other leg again, I saw that they had difficulty in walking and yet tried to maintain an erstwhile pride. They would be about seventy or so.

It proved a moving and comical sight to see them mill about the patiently laughing De Waeterlinck and jostle for the right to hold the floor. I didn't like it that De Waeterlinck continued to smile and nod like that. A certain remoteness is part of the face. Next time, I would have to sit closer to see if it was real. One must be meticulous with regard to faces.

The slight man held the floor. He looked aristocratic. While De Waeterlinck seemed to be listening attentively, and he also encouraged the man by nodding to him, I suddenly saw his glance shoot, in several short bursts, into the auditorium. It startled me, for even now it happened unexpectedly, but I did know what I had to do.

He saw me and immediately directed his gaze back to the speaker again. A moment later he looked into the hall once more and this time I was prepared. He looked at me. I looked back. This was an encounter, the beginning of a game.

I had time a-plenty. I had a future for all the Wednesdays of winter 1982.

There is no first time for seeing the face. The first time has always already been and is irretrievable. It is a man's face. It does not become much older than fifty and then it stays like that. Those men who have it bore it along with them as children, you can tell. It is craggy. Just to give the idea: Richard Burton, Ludwig Wittgenstein, Samuel Beckett, Lucas Asbeek and Witold Gombrowicz had it.

As did Marius. With Marius, I touched, caressed, perhaps also loved it for the first time. I was seventeen and he forty-eight. He taught sociology.

He was the second man from whom I received a book on philosophy as a present. It was a Prisma paperback with Plato's *Dialogues*. He said the point of it was the *Apologia* which I had to read; then I would get to know him better.

Since then, many men have given me books and doing so have said that it was a book through which I would get to know them better. They recognised themselves in the hero and believed they resembled him.

This was a mistake, usually.

For the first time, I read the story of Socrates' conviction. When I see Marius walking through the corridor at school and later see him standing in front of the class, I also see Socrates.

Marius can laugh so much about me that tears pour down his face.

'Did Socrates laugh so much, too,' I ask him, 'about a girl?'

When he gets to school in the morning he has bags under his eyes. Not through laughing. I pursue him through the building for as long as it takes until I see a chance to drag him into some place where I have him to myself. Toilets, broom cupboards, box rooms, storage spaces, empty class-rooms.

'You're upset,' I say to him and I touch the bags under his eyes.

'Lovey,' he says, 'what on earth are you doing? What do you want? What are you to do with an old codger like me?'

No one has ever said that to me before: 'lovey'.

Then he has to laugh. We are standing among the brooms, buckets and dishcloths. It smells of *Vim* there. He thinks it very exciting. So do I.

Ever more frequently I'm too late for class.

I go to school earlier each time. He waits for me in the car in a car park in the school's vicinity. I arrive on my bike from the village ten kilometres further out. I throw the bike down on the verge and run to the car.

In the mornings he's shattered. He's in the middle of a divorce. It's the first time I hear somebody speak about divorce. There's no divorcing in the village where I live. Divorce is for townies.

When it's cold, he leaves the engine running and he rubs the warmth back into my frozen hands. Sometimes he puts a blanket over my thighs. I let him talk and rest in my lap, caress his head, gently knead his neck. He has the compact body that befits the face. It has remained untouched for a long time. I want to do him good. I want to make him forget the suffering of the past evening.

'You're so haptic,' he said.

He frequently uses words of which I don't know the meaning and which I have to look up in the dictionary at home.

He caresses me too, very carefully. When he touches me it is as if he seeks the outline of an image which he knows and wants to find again. He has shaped his hands to my contours in advance and then he finds me. I fit them well, his hands. It makes me calm. I am not afraid. These are touchings without wildness, without desire.

He never needs to ask me to keep silent about us. I am used to having secrets.

When I am sitting in his class and he is teaching, he looks uninterruptedly at me. It is as if he speaks only for me. Everyone is aware of it but no one dares speak to me about it.

Once his wife has left him, we also occasionally see one another in the evening hours. After school, he takes me to the docks in the city where he teaches me to drink, and to expensive restaurants where he teaches me to dine. Wine, whisky, snails, frogs' legs, Coquilles St Jacques, lobster. It didn't start with him, that indissoluble link between eating and learning, eating and men, eating and love. This, too, began earlier on.

One day he says: 'You're very intelligent.'

I don't believe it. 'Intelligent' is my brothers' word. The elder knows the encyclopaedia off by heart and my younger brother ponders the boundlessness of the universe. That's the meaning of 'intelligent', it's the boys' word.

'You'll have to face up to it,' he says. He tells me about how the school is co-operating with the university in research and that a number of psychologists will be visiting to try out a new intelligence test. He wants me to take part in it. He wants me to go on and study, at university, yonder, in the West.

I think he wants to get rid of me and I tell him that I refuse to take part in the test and also that I don't want to go to university. I tell him that I'm not capable of it anyway, and that I like things very much as they are, with him, learning all sorts of things from him. He says he's an old codger and that I must look further ahead than just today, that life is still ahead of me and that I can do whatever I want.

'Tell me what you really want the most,' he says.

'To write books,' I say softly, out of embarrassment.

If that's what I want, I must get away from here, he says, away from him, away from the South, then I must get to know other men, see other cities, I must dare to tackle the dialogue with my own freedom. That otherwise nothing'll come of that writing of mine.

He makes me cry.

At the end of the evening he takes me home. I have promised him to take part in the test.

The test takes an entire day. I am frightened again and again at each new part of it, and am screamingly nervous. He sees something in me which I'm not. He's allowing himself to be deceived by my grades, but I make such high grades because the syllabus is so easy at this school. I would have been caught out a long time ago at other schools and the results of the test will prove this to him.

Even he is shaken by the result.

The psychologists have enclosed a brochure in which are the names of great scientists and writers. Behind these it says what percentage of the world's population they represent.

After this, he calls me: 'My little Einstein.'

He is proud. I am not. That strange number will chase me out into the world, away from him. I conceal it as though it were a disease.

Following De Waeterlinck's first lecture, I made sure I was in H 211 as early as possible. No matter how early I did come in, those elderly people would always be earlier, keeping the first row reserved for one another.

I did not dare to sit too near them and for the first few weeks I kept myself some metres away. Each week I would choose the same place in order to savour the delight of seeing De Waeterlinck's gaze go in my direction on entering. First he would nod amiably to the front row and then he would look at me. He was looking for me and I was there. I was always there.

In order not to have to miss the crossing of our glances for a single instance, I would make hardly any notes and would stare at his face continuously. Without having to look down on to the page, I tried, without looking, to write down the titles of books, the names of their authors or a few striking comments. I became very proficient at this.

At times I think he is speaking about us. He is talking about Ficino's philosophy and he remarks how important a look is for a sense of love and happiness.

'Contrary to taste and touch,' he says, 'both the ear and the eye require distance. The eye and the ear do not use anything up, they do not consume, they do not gobble you up. The eye and the ear are therefore essentially melancholy and full of death-wish. The look of a loved one can chain you, but while it does so, it sets you free at the same time. It suffuses you with the shiver of the magic of love, but it continues to be observational, at a distance. It is the look which respects the other's loneliness, which has a sense of otherness and at the same time it is content with itself. In Ficino, an indissoluble link is forged between sight, love and thought. You would have to have been madly in love to be able to make a start on thought.'

The last months of the year acquired the colour of these Wednesday-morning lectures. When I walked outside I would look around me in the hope of running into De Waeterlinck in the wild. At home, in my room, I read the books about which he had spoken but the reading of the books itself had to take second place to the way in which the texts had been distorted by De Waeterlinck, had been mixed in by him with other texts, his own concerns and encased in those extraordinary Flemish words.

On Wednesday mornings I would dress differently from what was my wont. I had not worn skirts for years. The moment I happened to put one on again, I felt as if I was undergoing a kind of cross-dressing and was disguising myself as a woman. This strange, improper feeling of being dressed-up quite suited me for the visits to the lectures, and for the first time in years I exchanged my trousers and jacket for a skirt beneath which I wore nylons and high-heeled shoes. I felt provocative and began to walk in a different manner because of this.

The elderly people's curiosity increased. When I entered the lecture theatre or remained in my seat during the interval, they would look me up and down in ever more blatant gazes. In time, one of the women became even more crass and, when De Waeterlinck kept his eyes trained on me for longer than normal, would regularly turn round altogether, follow the line of his gaze and stare at me quite shamelessly. She was the same woman who would hand De Waeterlinck a paper bag during every interval, probably containing a buttered roll. Without fail, the package would be gratefully accepted by him and subsequently put aside.

I never did see him eat a roll during the interval.

I watched from my seat in the hall and kept silent. Occasionally I would go outside with the others during the interval. On those occasions I wouldn't have the courage to stay put.

A few weeks before the beginning of the Christmas holidays I noticed that my role was beginning to bore me. I would have to undertake something, become more real, come closer, get acquainted, begin to speak, gain a name for myself. This intention made me so nervous that I would get palpitations at times when De Waeterlinck looked at me. For the first time I took refuge in making notes so that our gazes would meet less frequently.

That was the way it went during the last lecture of that year, too.

It was freezing cold outside and there had been warnings of slippery roads. I went to school on foot. From the bridge, immediately in front of the entrance gate into the university campus, I saw how a taxi driver was helping one of the elderly people get out of the car. He was supporting her arm and holding her walking stick ready for her. She was the tall woman with the red hair. She was wearing a fur coat. With a careful shuffling gait she passed underneath the entrance archway so that I lost sight of her. The foremost part of the entrance was not covered. It was likely to be just as slippery there as on other roads.

As quickly as possible, I made for the archway and thought about how I would greet her and offer her my arm, but when I turned the corner I saw she was already receiving help from the man with the long grey hair. They had progressed but a few metres and I checked my step. He was wearing a woolly hat on the back of his head and had linked his arm in hers. They were completely absorbed in the taking of their hesitant little steps and tested the ground with their feet. For a moment I felt something like disappointment because I saw a fine opportunity to get acquainted slip away and I didn't believe any more either that I would be able to free myself, under my own steam, without the old people's intercession, of my own inaccessibility and thus come into contact with De Waeterlinck.

I did not dare to pass them and I continued to walk behind them with what was for me unaccustomed tardiness.

Before they entered the covered section of the corridor I suddenly saw them together like on a photograph on which the entrance to the passage encased them like a frame. The image filled me with pity. These were old people, they took the risk of being out of doors on a day like this, they exposed their brittle bones to the danger of a fatal fall, just to come and listen to the professor. Would they, at seventy, still be going round with the same questions as I did, would they still hanker after knowledge, still be searching for a voice sounding clearer than the one of that maundering adversary in one's own head? Would it actually never stop, ever?

In the new year, the lectures started again on a miserable, wet Wednesday morning in January. It was dark and cold rain was coming down. I put on my leather jacket and my hat. It was a brown man's hat, a Borsalino, which I had picked up for little money and which, since the first time I had put it on, I had begun to regard as being indispensable.

'Your attire is your *pneuma*,' De Waeterlinck had once

said during a lecture and it does sound quite pretty but I don't believe it. Turn up your collar, put a hat on your head and from one moment to the next you have the unapproachable soul of an Italian mafia boss. With clothes it's the same thing as with words; they're ready-made, secondhand, laden with massiveness and history, impossible instruments for the purely personal – if it actually exists, that is.

With Don Corleone's *pneuma* and my own timorous heart, I strode to school and read on the notice board in the hallway that De Waeterlinck's lectures would no longer be held in H 211 but in another room, on the first floor. I took the stairs and made my way unsuspecting to the door bearing the relevant number. I expected everything to have stayed as it was before and all the rooms in the building to be identical, but when I cast a glance inside I saw to my horror a completely different kind of space. The floor wasn't raked. In the middle of the classroom there was a table around which the old people thronged. I looked straight into the eyes of the man with the grey hair.

'And here she is,' he said and he made a broad, theatrical, sweeping gesture with his arm.

'What a splendid hat, my dear, quite splendid. Do sit down. Here.'

I entered with a furtive laugh and took the seat the man had indicated. The other elderly people nodded at me amiably and began to say something all at once so I didn't understand a word. The only one who was silent and clenched his narrow lips was the small, tawny man. He took me in with a penetrating gaze and did not acknowledge my nod in greeting but again bent over the book he was reading. I didn't dare to look anyone in the eye at any real length and allowed myself to be taken in tow by the stream of words of the man with the long hair. He was going on about the hat and the way I had come in.

'Splendid entrance, my dear,' he said, 'irresistible, a consummate actress. I'm a silly old man, but I see things. The way you came in like that, the hat drawn down deeply over your eyes, unforgettable, truly unforgettable.'

'You damn fool, you,' the woman with the red hair said.

Another woman tugged at my sleeve and said best to take no notice of him. 'Perfectly crackers,' she said in a heavy German accent. She had parchment skin with pale liver-spots on her cheeks and a few larger discolourations on her forehead. The woman of the packed lunches. She sat with her face turned towards the door. From the beaming eyes I could glean that De Waeterlinck was now entering the room. I braced myself.

The table we were sitting at had been slid up against the one behind which De Waeterlinck would be taking his seat. I had never seen him at such close quarters; I could almost smell him.

My sudden proximity startled him. He regarded me with a surprised look, nodded and then he greeted the old people.

The fatal woman, as does every myth, has a vested interest in distance. If you really must be a mystery, you have to keep out of the way of those you wish to seduce by being veiled. The moment you abolish distance and fill the void with yourself, there is nothing more for the myth-maker to invent.

My proximity was downright murder of the female figure of fiction.

My name's not Carmen, Rosa Fröhlich or Natasia Phillipovna.

Those are the women from stories and I don't resemble them remotely. But even characters you have nothing in common with force their way in, subtly, and turn some moments in your life into a scene in which you act according to an age-old scenario and you hear yourself utter sentences of which you know for sure that at one time they have been spoken by someone else and have had their effect.

The old people's liveliness had simplified the abandoning of the scenario of the last three months. I felt myself to have been taken up and I couldn't be bothered that now I could foresee no longer how things would turn out.

Professor De Waeterlinck went over to the switch and clicked on the lights in the hall. He took his seat behind the table and sighed deeply. As in the previous lectures there was no sheet of paper on his table.

Behind the woman with the German accent, two students were still embroiled in lively conversation. She turned round and ordered them to be silent. Even her 'Sshht' sounded German.

De Waeterlinck wished us a happy New Year and said that today we were altogether too literally cloaked in darkness.

'Be that as it may, we will continue to search for a way out. It's worth the effort to continue even so.'

Now that I was sitting so close, I was able to study De Waeterlinck's face and I wondered whether I had been mistaken. Wasn't there something missing in the face which was absolutely indispensable, but which it was impossible for me to say what it needed to be? Would I, in him, find what I was searching for, the thing for which I didn't have a word but which had something to do with the way in which Marius handled me at the time?

Marius would notice immediately when I was cold, would take off his coat and, without saying a word, would put it across my shoulders. Marius would look forward to choosing the food for me and he relished watching me when I encountered a new taste. Marius would bombard me with advice such as: 'You need more armour on your soul' and 'You must also learn to talk about the weather'. Marius said that a writer must be able to be alone, that in a good novel everything is bound up with everything else, that modern literature now can only have language itself for its subject, that intelligent people never marry, that you must look into each other's eyes when you raise your glasses in a toast and that the twentieth century was not to be compared with any other century because men had been to the moon. Marius needed me.

It was open to question whether De Waeterlinck was sufficiently unhappy to be able to bear my solace. Now I was taking a better look, I began to doubt precisely that. There was something lacking in his eyes, a yearning, a hopeless longing, overt panic like that I always saw in Marius' eyes and which sometimes, for a moment, I was able to dispel. More than this I didn't have to offer, I thought, and if I wasn't able to give him even so little, it would be pointless to be elected his chosen one.

De Waeterlinck told about how he had spent his Christmas recess.

'I whiled away the hours the entire time with modern, French philosophers. These are truly most refined, whizzy-dizzy texts, but each time the feeling steals up on me that it was all thought up long before them, by Hegel and other nineteenth century philosophers. Hegel in particular has had to endure some uncommonly hard knocks from these French exegetists, and at times this is painful to have to read. I am familiar with the growing popularity of the French here at the university, but I hope you will continue to be capable of seeing, through all that clumsy misinterpretation, the philosophy of Hegel himself, for example, and to allow it to evolve alongside during your encounter with all this modern heritage of thought.

'A truly original spirit will wish to innovate and in order to innovate there has to be some tearing down, clearly. But that which is meant to be torn down must, thank heavens, first be studied and known thoroughly; you too must do this first. I personally, after ten years of French philosophy, have become more nineteenth century than ever before.' He stopped for a moment and then added forcefully: 'And I shall continue to be, too!'

'Bravo!' cried the old man with the grey hair and clapped his hands a few times. While doing so he looked at me, laughing, and expected me to join him in his enthusiasm which, of course, I did not.

The old people all had an exercise book lying in front of them and during De Waeterlinck's introduction they had busily been taking down notes. From where I was sitting, I could not see the tawny man without bending across the table top. This I did not do. I had the feeling he was keeping an eye on me. I did now see lying there the book which he had been reading when I came in. Goethe's poetry.

De Waeterlinck took up the subject of the lecture again: Schopenhauer's aesthetics. I was relieved he ceased his attack on the French philosophers and did not touch upon them again.

I was very impressed by Foucault.

I was quite gaga about Foucault.

At times I dreamed of him.

A few years ago, after a ramble through France, my friend the astrologer had brought back a book for me. He had taken advice from a friend in Paris whom he frequently stayed with. Foucault, *Les mots et les choses*, that friend had said. Since that time, I had always continued to be curious as to who the man was who had selected precisely this philosopher for me.

As was the case more often, having read the book, I believed that my life would now change completely. I had never clapped eyes on anything like it. I would love to have thought something similar myself, and to have written it. Mr Foucault wrote philosophy in a style which was just as exciting as that of a novel. It was unclear whether a poet or a philosopher was speaking.

Mr Foucault had a grip on the soul of my generation, a generation after Mr Sartre or the gentlemen of the *Frankfurter Schule*. The soul they spoke of was already dated when my generation perforce had to inherit it because there was nothing else to hand. I have always held Mr Sartre in high esteem for he was the first philosopher I read a book by. And though the Sartrian soul was a heavy one to bear, it gave me much pleasure for it was a modern soul, a soul of the twentieth century. Any other soul was outdated, in my opinion, and to be outdated seemed stupid to me, so I was proudly free and responsible and I was highly surprised when I heard someone defend determinism and inheritance by generations, for belief in a kind of doom did not agree with the belief of the twentieth century. I wondered how anyone could be so old-fashioned, and in the main I stuck with the idea that the defenders of determinism had not yet read the right books.

Compared with the Sartrian soul, Mr Foucault's was light and airy-fairy. With shame I would at times read descriptions of behaviour I myself displayed, of thoughts which I believed had welled up spontaneously in me but of which Mr Foucault maintained that these were actions and ideas you were unnoticeably forced towards by language and by science. Personality was just as big a myth as Mr Sartre's freedom and, as there was nothing I desired more than to have a personality, I was much relieved to think that such a

80

thing did not exist at all, perhaps, and I could occupy myself with other matters.

I was glad that Mr Foucault did not want me to be as free as Mr Sartre did, and with a sense of relief and enlightenment I swapped my old soul for a new one. Determinism was not so bad, after all.

The woman with the German accent had pointedly looked at her watch a few times already and now she was tapping her finger nail on the glass, by means of which she was trying to draw De Waeterlinck's attention. He understood her directions, nodded to her and wound up his tale in such a way that he could herald the start of the interval.

How could he so thoughtlessly give heed to the petty tyranny of a woman, I wondered. Did he let himself be pushed around? Was he docile? Did he, as long as he was among people, continually engage in compromises so that he was then forced to flee from everybody in order to protect himself against their greed?

Now that I was noticing at close quarters the small exchanges of glances, the facial tics (he would repeatedly clench the muscles surrounding his left eye and at times his lower lip trembled) and his meekness, the myth of which Daniel had spoken lost its sheen.

De Waeterlinck was not intractable – he was too tractable. I had hoped this was not to prove to be so, but in fact I had already seen enough. And if I was right and he was indeed someone who had few means of defence against the world and who had to hide in order to be able to be honest, then he was one of my kind and our kind at best had compassion but rarely great admiration for its fellows.

Not in any way did this diminish my excitement at what might happen during the interval, however.

The room emptied. The man with the long, grey hair stood up and with a deep bow and a flourish of his arm introduced himself as Aaron Mendes da Costa. He presented the red-haired woman like a fellow actor in a play. He pointed her out and called her 'my dear, dear friend Katherina Riwalski'. She remained seated but laughing held out a slender hand to me while apologising for not being able to get up because her legs functioned badly. He pronounced the name of the woman with the German accent incorrectly ('Ida') at which point she corrected him with a mixture of tartness and understanding and introduced herself with a powerful handshake as being Ilda Müller. Following this, she delved into her handbag, retrieved a paper bag and walked towards De Waeterlinck. I began to fear that things would go wrong.

The little man who was reading Goethe's poetry upon my arrival had gone straight over to De Waeterlinck and was standing there with his back turned to us. It felt like a rejection of my interfering. I thought to read from the attitude of his shoulders that he was irritated by the noisiness of our little group and that he also was trying to block De Waeterlinck's way to us. The man called Mendes da Costa did indeed speak in a loud voice and a declamatory manner, funny and unceasing. Now and again I would look at De Waeterlinck and saw that he, too, was glancing over the shoulder of the little man to look our way. Then he would direct his gaze back toward the man who continued to stand right in front of him and I looked back at Mendes da Costa again.

It would also have gone wrong had Aaron Mendes da Costa not been so grandiose and less intuitive. Probably, he had cottoned on to it from the very first moment I allowed myself to be distracted from his performance to look at De Waeterlinck, but had postponed the moment at which he presented himself as a seer because he enjoyed his own tales far too much. Just before the end of the interval, he said he knew what I was after. 'You don't need to tell me anything, my dear,' he said, 'I can see. My tales bore you and you'd dearly like something else. Come.'

While talking, he walked up to De Waeterlinck and the little man, wished them a happy New Year, and with much bravura introduced me to Guido de Waeterlinck and to the man who was called László Kovács.

'I would very much like to make an appointment with you,' I said to De Waeterlinck, 'I should like to sit a prelim.'

At the conclusion of the second period, Mendes da Costa proposed that all of us should go and have some coffee downstairs in the canteen. The others rather liked the idea too, except for László Kovács: he was not coming. From that time on, I followed professor De Waeterlinck's lectures till the end of my studies and spent Wednesday afternoons in the colourful company of Aaron Mendes da Costa, Katherina Riwalski and Ilda Müller. One day, László Kovács left and never came back.

Aaron became my oldest friend and he was an inspired storyteller. He could hold forth for entire afternoons on end without allowing himself to be interrupted by others. Without fail, his stories would begin with the announcement that this was to be a lengthy affair, then he would recount an incident and say: 'This was the introduction – end of the first tale', accompanying this with a circling movement of his graceful hands, like a conductor concluding a final bar. This would be followed by an anecdote with at its centre a completely different incident, which he would wind up with the remark: 'End of the second tale', finally, often much too hastily because of his own enthusiasm for a splendid plot, to tell his third tale in which the characters from the first and second tale meet by accident and prove to be made for one another. 'Lovely story, what?' he would then ask, and when I nodded he would say: 'Yes, my dear, I have had a curious life.'

In Aaron's tales everything always turned out well in the end.

A few days after my introduction to the old people, I ran into László Kovács in the university library. He was descending the stairs with a number of books under his left arm and I was climbing them in order to change a similar number, at least, for other ones. I had resolved to take my first degree before the end of the winter and had agreed with De Waeterlinck to sit my final oral with him in a fortnight's time.

Having made the appointment, I felt better. I had gently detached myself and the others from the rigidity which the fantasist out of necessity imposes on himself and on the characters who have to play a part in it. As unpredictable as real dreams are, the imaginings made by daylight are immutable. The fantasist embodies in his fantasies the same character each time: hero, victim, *femme fatale*, genius, master, and for the changing players acting opposite, too, the roles available vary little. Heroes have the opportunity of a lifetime and are admired by their opponents, victims get a hiding and solace, the *femme fatale* is desired to distraction and then drives the lover to ruin, the genius is recognised and the master finds a slave.

Now that I had become acquainted with everybody and had given up organising coincidence, life could again continue on its own capricious way.

Kovács peered intently at the treads of the stairs and every time stood with both feet on a tread before stepping down onto the next one. When I know someone's face I cannot simply pass them by without greeting them and so I said something to Kovács on my way up. He looked up, irked. Until now I had only seen him talking and listening, during which his face had borne an expression of gravity and concentration, a little gruff, too, and grudging.

With a short, fierce glance he observed me and a surprised smile appeared around his narrow mouth. The smile changed his face completely and I had a great sense of relief, as if I had withstood a test.

'Scervusc,' he said and put out his right hand to me. In meticulous and almost accent-free Dutch he asked me immediately which books I had on me, which ones I intended to borrow next and then he said that I certainly must read the book he was now taking home with him a second time, an utterly hilarious listing of research results, faulty interpretations and miscalculations which had been swept under the carpet and which had led to great discoveries in science.

Surprised at the enthusiasm with which he asked me questions and told of his own reading pleasure, I leaned against the banister one tread lower down than he.

We both seemed to forget where we were and I did not see his gaze wander a single time. It was permanently directed at my face, scrutinising it while he spoke.

Looking up like this gave me a crick in the neck and in the end I proposed to go and have a cup of coffee somewhere or to continue our conversation some other time.

From the start, I feared this would not go down with him very well. His face at once assumed an insulted expression. He looked at his watch and said that in that case we had better chat some other time for he still had to go somewhere.

Taking leave, he did his best to smile but he couldn't really manage it.

I could.

'You are so familiar to me,' Guido de Waeterlinck said after the prelim, 'it is as if I have known you for years.'

I told him I felt the same.

He was sitting back in his chair, relaxed. Of the nervousness he had shown at the beginning of the prelim nothing remained. It had been on the cards for him to give me a high mark and at the end of the inquisition propose that we leave his office and have a drink in some hostelry or other. His working day was done and we ought to get to know each other better, he had said, certainly now I had honoured him with the request to tutor me during the writing of my thesis.

In the café, I asked him what truth there was in the tale about him that was doing the rounds, about the burning of his work and his aversion to writing.

'It's the same as with the misanthropist,' he said. 'He loves people too much so he is permanently being betrayed and contrariwise develops a hate for his greatest object of love. The tale has been embellished, of course. I burned nothing. I only put a great quantity of waste paper by the dustbin and it was truly a liberation, a cleansing of my spirit. Some insights happen to be accompanied by agonies, pain and the destruction of the old. My insight was to be a servant, not a master. My love for language is too big, I love it too much to see it turn to mould through blunt syntax the moment I take up a pen, and to be stretched between this unfortunate dichotomy of my spirit which seeks to make me be both artist and thinker. I am neither and as such have found myself out. I am a servant of language, the writers are my prompters and I recite their words. To know how to die is the final secret of every initiation and I am at peace with having come to this synthesis. I'm a reader, a speaker, an actor, nothing more. Direct contact with the audience is indispensable to me.

'According to me, you possess something which I utterly

lack, but which probably is a precondition for practising every form of art, a kind of synthesis between passion and detachment. There is in you something of anger and compassion, a longing to master the masters in a gentle way.'

'Is that so? How d'you know?' I asked.

'I have watched you,' he said. 'You have contained the tension a long time, but now the battle is being fought before my eyes. You have conquered the hearts of my most loyal audience and I see that they move you the way they move me. Almost all of them are refugees and thanks to them I often have the feeling of being connected to history, still to be able to assuage some of the suffering endured. Doubtlessly, this is the emotional state of a neurotic human being who cannot achieve a reconciliation between the contradictions of life and is weighed down by continual feelings of guilt. You do not act because of guilt. Something else drives you.'

'What's that then?'

'I don't know. You should be telling me.' But I did not know either, not really.

'It was pleasant to speak with you like this,' Guido had said on parting, and asked if we might do it again some time.

'As often as you like,' I answered.

It would also turn out to be Guido who warned me about taking Lászlo Kovács's feelings seriously.

As for clichés – I once fixed it firmly in my head that they are to be avoided. No doubt Marius, at some time, will have said something like: 'The cliché is the death of literature, a sign of a dearth of language and a lack of originality', and this law was confirmed by the literary criticism I read later on.

That's why I avoided them assiduously until I came into contact with Lászlo Kovács and discovered that there is something worse wrong with a bromide than just its apparent disfiguring of language.

For a long time I used to think that people allowed themselves to be led by their will, by their passions, convictions and ideas, by something in themselves, but since getting to know Lászlo I have become convinced more and more that we are not spurred by our passions, but by the tropes of passion and that it isn't pure will that spurs us to action but the clichés about will. Only when experience coincides with the cliché of what is a true experience, and we can shelter in the safety of language, does something like a sense of truthfulness come into being, the idea of being right, of existing truly, of being real.

Lászlo Kovács allowed himself to be led by the cliché that a man is as old as he feels. Lászlo Kovács was seventy-four when I met him, but Lászlo Kovács felt himself to be eighteen.

Aaron and Guido both had a premonition of subsequent developments, but I have never been able to check this because I was ashamed and did not speak with them about Lászlo after he had left.

Aaron saw himself as being the perfect opposite of Lászlo.

'I'm a braggart,' he said, 'and of course I, too, desire you, but were you to ask me if I really want something to happen: no. I'm a foolish man, but I do still have an eye for reality. Kovács is different, fiercer, more passionate, more unrealistic perhaps, who can tell. He wants you, period. It's all a matter of resisting death, no doubt. You don't need to tell me anything, my dear, I know alright. You call us back to life, no messing about. But isn't it a splendid

88

story, two such old goats who tie themselves in knots for a single second of your attention, a glimpse of your naughty eyes and a kiss from your rose-red mouth.'

Sentences such as these were uttered ironically by Aaron. He would then strongly emphasise the tone of artificiality, speaking slowly, and with his full lips he would shape the words with exaggerated gravity.

He was right, though. László wanted me – all of me.

Following our encounter in the library, he had joined us in the interval during the next lecture and had also walked along with the others to the canteen afterwards. He had barely spoken a word, but had regularly looked me in the face, searchingly. This recurred for a number of weeks. It was clear he was not enjoying it.

On one of those Wednesdays, arriving back home, I found a folded note inside my bag. There was no envelope round it.

The note was László's. He proposed meeting in the canteen an hour before the lecture began so that we would be able to conduct a proper conversation and were not buried beneath the high-jinks of the mass-meeting after the lecture. At the bottom of the letter he had put his address and I wrote back to him that this was fine with me. In the hours prior to the lecture I never got down to anything anyway.

From that time onwards I sat on Wednesday morning from ten to a quarter past eleven opposite László at a table. Unlike Aaron, he did not like to hear himself speak and no one has ever asked me so many questions as did László Kovács. Do you often fall in love? With what kind of men? Does a man have to be attractive to you? Do men evoke sexual desire in you? Who? How? When? Is your desire influenced by anything, hormones, films, reading matter? Does a man need to be passionate with you or, on the contrary, reticent in fact? What does love mean to you? Try that lot for size.

The unfamiliarity with the questions, the genuine interest with which he posed them and his own openness when I in my turn asked him questions, gave me a feeling of safety and I practised giving as honest answers as possible, something which cost me much effort. But I trusted him, and I trusted his interpretations above all.

László did not regale me with how sweet, friendly, soft, caring, spontaneous, cheerful, sensitive, intelligent and honest I happened to be, something I can never endure without having the feeling that someone had fallen for it again and not fathomed my true nature, of which I, too, hadn't a clue as to what it looked like but about which I suspected the worst. László unhesitatingly said that I was impenetrable, haughty, coquettish, aggressive, obsessional, melancholic, pessimistic, suspicious, destructive, megalomaniacal, inaccessible and narcissistic. My longing for love he stamped as being *selige Sehnsucht*, my love motto as being *und wenn ich dich liebe, was geht es dich an*, and my true loves as being rare curios because I loved like the men of the tribe of Asra, *welche sterben, wenn sie lieben*.

I believed him.

He tried to understand why I was made the way I was.

I looked forward to our meetings. Between Wednesdays we would write letters ever more frequently, in due course several each week even. The opening line to his letters was the same as the greeting with which he would be waiting for me on Wednesday mornings: 'Scervusc kislany.' It meant something like 'nice girl', he had said. He signed himself with 'the bolond', meaning 'old fool', but which I never used to address him by because I would then have to deprive my tongue of the unusual acrobatics when, with a whiplash, it tried to form his proper name.

László said, wrote and cried that he was in love, but I thought there was no harm in this, that it was something he himself relished without in fact needing me for it. After all, Aaron, too, regularly recited declarations of love, and according to him I had even enchanted Ilda Müller.

'What's the most beautiful film, post-war?' he once had asked her bluntly when we were sitting in the canteen.

'*Mädchen in Uniform*,' she said, without hesitating.

'Shush now,' Aaron had said, 'no need to say a word.' He had then put his hand on her lower arm. The moment was solemn and I was sure that their quick exchange reached further than me and touched upon a covenant between themselves, a shared past, a history, a time in which I was unborn. The same way I would also listen to László's declarations of love, as if they did not concern me but something bigger and more impersonal, something past.

László persisted, doggedly, convinced. He wanted my love. The tone of our conversations became more tart, his letters turned into accusations, mine into rejections and defences. He remembered everything, pursued me with my answers, interpreted each glance, touch, comma and full-stop; he interpreted each word and every time differently from what I had meant, I said, I wrote.

'You charm everyone and never allow yourself to be charmed,' he said.

'If you leave me, that would be a retrospective reaction to your relationship with Marius,' he said.

'Stop banging on like that,' I said. 'Stop desiring me. You make me nervous. You're not realistic.'

Our letters ended up being interpretations of interpretations and eventually I no longer dared to tackle my own sentences and reacted for a week on end with only quotations.

With Kierkegaard, when he reproached me with having created the impression with my behaviour of desiring him completely, too:

Mann erfährt aus dem Tagebuch, dass es mitunter etwas ganz Willkürliches war, das er begehrte, zum Beispiel einen Gruss, und um keinen Preis mehr annehmen wollte, weil es das Schönste bei der Betreffenden war.

With Kafka, when he wrote that I was capricious and unpredictable:

Ich ruhe eben nicht in mir, ich bin nicht immer "etwas" und wenn ich einmal "etwas" war, bezahle ich es mit dem "Nichtsein" von Monaten.

These were the last letters. One Tuesday morning in April I received a picture postcard.

'Limit. Resigned. Won't be there tomorrow and will no longer bother you. The bolond.'

Chapter IV

THE PRIEST

It is a Sunday afternoon in March, 1983, when I ring at
Clemens Brandt's door. I press the folder with papers hard
into my side. It's too late now to think up a variant of the
hackneyed greeting which I keep rehearsing for myself. I
can hardly say to him that the world makes sense to me in
an elegant way because today's Sunday and he's a priest
and they belong to one another; that, now I have ended up
here anyway, I couldn't have thought up any other day for
meeting him.

After I've pressed the bell-push I wipe my right hand on
my skirt and try to keep it dry for as long as possible.

Brandt is famous. That he was once ordained a priest, I
only discovered when I had already made an appointment
with him and hurriedly borrowed from the university the
only book by him I hadn't read yet. It was his first, the
publication of his doctoral thesis. In his later books there
was never mention made of any priesthood in the bio-
graphical entry.

I could not grasp writer and priest in one. I had not run
into a priest in years. The image I kept had been coloured
in solitude by the parish priest in the village of my birth.

Priests have a vocation, a housekeeper and wax-pale
hands. In the morning they preach in church, they baptise,

marry, hear confession and only visit people in their homes when they are having children or are dying. In the main, they keep silent. They read and pray. They always read the same book and in due course they know it off by heart. They are different from our fathers. They are not normal men.

To conduct a conversation with an author was creepy, though not impossible. To conduct a conversation with a priest *was* impossible. What was Clemens Brandt? You cannot be a priest and a writer at the same time: the one is a deviation of the other, in a way. Either Clemens Brandt was an abnormal priest or an abnormal writer.

The door is large and heavy relative to the man who opens it. He is small, fat and has an all-dominating head with bloodhound-cheeks, double chins and a bulging, pointed pate on which long hair has been plastered down in greasy strands. The spectacles on his nose have a heavy frame and the lenses are murky with grime.

He is the ugliest man I have ever seen.

In an unexpectedly sonorous voice he invites me in. It's not a case of ugly men not being allowed to have a fine voice, not at all, it's just another disproportion brought to light by this, a chasm between his eyes and this vocal sound, these soft, tender, deep sounds. Those eyes aren't like that.

When I shake his hand, and drone through my sentence, an acute boredom creeps into his expression, an undisguised aversion to sentences of greeting which he has perhaps been forced to listen to hundreds of times before. It shakes me. He made no attempt whatsoever to conceal his resentment and to feign that it was the first time he had heard someone express her admiration and respect.

I curse my manners and lack of daring, and I decide to sail a radically different course. All that humbleness never gets you anywhere.

He takes my coat and turns his back on me to hang it on a peg. Then, unexpectedly, I see a shadow in a spot where there shouldn't be a shadow, somewhere between his shoulderblades. It's a hump.

He opens one of the doors leading off from the hallway, asks me to go in ahead and take a seat while he'll make some coffee in the meantime.

In the sitting room, a silky feeling of compassion comes over me which attaches itself inside my throat and does not disappear for the time being. An open crochet-work tablecloth lies on a round table. I think that's the cause of it all.

The incoming light is being dimmed by tight-woven lace curtains made from a coarse material. An indescribable order reigns which is also continued in the heavy, oak bookcases against the wall. The bookcase doesn't make me curious but because I hesitate whether I should sit down at the table or on one of the settees set at right angles to one another in a different corner of the room, I go and stand bang in front of it. There's nothing to be gleaned from it. Clemens Brandt has the collected works of more or less everybody: Aristotle, Augustine, Hume, Hobbes, Hegel, Plato, everything.

In the hall the chink of china sounds. I tilt my head to one side and pretend to be busy reading the titles on the spines. I resolve not to make a single remark about his book collection.

Clemens Brandt comes in with a tray and walks over carefully to the low coffee table which stands near the settees. Besides a pile of new, by the looks of them still unread books, a big brown envelope with my handwriting on it is lying there too.

Guido said I deserved a better instructor, that as a hopeless

Hegelian and die-hard nineteenth-centuryist, he could not help me along any further.

'You are hopelessly in love with the twentieth century,' he said and he gave me the address of Clemens Brandt. He advised me to send my first degree thesis to him. I could not believe he uttered that name, actually said 'Clemens Brandt'.

'*The* Clemens Brandt, you mean?' I asked and that's the one he meant.

'I haven't written anything which Clemens Brandt hasn't written already in different words, or which he might have written,' I said to Guido. 'He is quoted on every fifth page of my piece and even if I do have ideas, these are developments of something he's left lying about somewhere.'

'That's just it,' Guido said. 'Because you admire Brandt as a writer you ascribe to him an originality you do not possess yourself. But his books, too, are developments of things left lying about by another author.'

I received a reply within a fortnight.

Groningen, March 25, 1983

Dear Miss M. Deniet,

Thank you so much for your kind letter and your thesis. I have read your effort critically and with interest. I believe I am able to say without further ado that this thesis offers a sufficient basis for a Master's thesis and even for possible publication in our periodical. I should like very much to exchange views with you on a number of points, though. To do this in writing would seem rather time consuming, however, but I would gladly meet with you at some time in order to discuss these different matters with you in person. Should you ever have the opportunity to come North at some point, you will be most welcome. An appointment by telephone would be desirable.

There is one point I should still like to raise here. The relationship between philosophy and literature has been a most particular interest of mine for many years. It is not clear to me from your thesis, nor perhaps in Foucault's case, what is the difference between a text as such and what is called a literary text. Put differently, what makes literature literature?

Yours, with kind regards,
Prof. C. Brandt.

Of the tension, nervousness and excitement which I had had after reading the letter, there was nothing left now. I sat on the settee opposite Clemens Brandt, within the four walls of his living room and this seemed the most ordinary thing in the world to me. It appeared to me as if nothing could happen I wasn't prepared for, for Brandt wasn't a strange creature, no member of a secret society to which I had no entrance, no participant in a game of which I could not fathom the rules. Brandt was an earthly, normal man, deformed it's true, but otherwise a man like others I knew. He looked at women in quite an impertinent manner. He looked at my mouth when I spoke and he looked at my knees when I was sitting opposite him. All fine and dandy. Everything about him that had seemed absurd and extraordinary before I met him, would have to be explained through something I had neither gleaned from his books nor from his biography: his deformity. The unexpected brazenness with which he divulged his boredom in the hallway and the sensuous way in which he now looked me up and down, without any attempt at concealing the direction of his glances from me, were at most puzzling in combination with his ugliness, but otherwise I did not expect unforeseen developments that Sunday.

97

I have misjudged things on other occasions too.

He poured coffee from a floral patterned pot, into some of those fragile Royal Albert cups. He did this very carefully and with concentration. There were some chocolate-tipped brandy snaps on a cut-glass little dish. After he had filled our cups he himself, without offering me any, took a biscuit first, bit into it eagerly and leaned back, his cup in his hand, into the settee. There were crumbs round his still full mouth when he slurped down some coffee. He looked me in the face as he did this. I laughed.

'Why do you laugh?' he asked.

'Because you slurp and guzzle,' I said, and I knew what I was doing.

For a second or so of turning to stone he stared at me, his eyes large with amazement. Then he laughed. He laughed, baring a row of big, strong, brown-yellow teeth between which remnants of chocolate could still be seen.

'You have written a fine piece, Miss Deniet,' he said. 'After I had read it, I thought of it frequently. You hadn't written your name in full anywhere and so I would think of "the piece by Miss Em". Just now, I heard that you have the same name as my mother's and, frankly, I suspected this already. Unless you object, I'll stick to Em.'

I didn't object, I was used to it. I told him so.

'I know it well,' he said. 'Psychologically speaking it's a strange thing, a name-change. I was baptised Petrus Hendrikus and was called Pete at home. As a Jesuit, in the end, I assumed the name of Clemens. I myself had opted for Gabriel, but that name was already spoken for.'

As he spoke, some spit would appear on his lips which subsequently he sucked inside again. This made him look very childlike, rather like a babe-in-arms. Strangely enough, I wasn't able to imagine him as a child, but to

98

realise that he once had been a boy who had listened to the name Peter or Pete, moved me.

I asked him whether he was still a priest.

'An apostate,' he said.

'What a shame,' I said. 'With a voice such as yours you would shake the faith of even the most dyed-in-the-wool atheist.'

He laughed loudly, with wide-opened mouth. He looked at me gratefully.

'It really is a fine piece, Miss Em. I must confess that though the style made me curious as to the writer, I did not have much faith in this meeting. The thing is temptingly written but very thoroughly too. This is why I had not expected a person such as yourself, more of a serious, rather stiff and certainly a somewhat older student. What great age are you now?'

'Twenty-seven and very serious indeed,' I replied with reluctance, for I preferred him to continue talking, to engage with the contents of my thesis, and finally to ask me the question he had put before me in the letter.

From the moment I caught sight of the question, I thought about it. I could not make an appointment by phone with Clemens Brandt before I believed I knew the answer. In order to arrive well-armed, I had written a new essay in which I had collected a great number of definitions by philosophers and writers and finally added one of my own. Recklessly, I had called it *This is Literature* and I hoped he would think it good enough to publish. It was in my bag. Brandt's invitation to exchange views on the basis of something I had written had filled me with pride. During the two-hour train journey I had endlessly repeated the conversation we would have, heard myself give astute replies, seen myself raise problems, hear his work surveyed critically and find in him a keen listener, wiser than I, indulgently correcting my bold inventions, then to be showered with unfamiliar authors, titles and fascinating thoughts.

To speak for yourself is easy – on your own.

If there was something Brandt did not feel like, it was the conversation I had already had with him in my imagination: I saw this in no time. He didn't want to talk with me about language, literature and philosophy at all, about why we call *Madame Bovary* a novel and *Ecce Homo* philosophy. Most of all, Brandt wanted to abandon as soon as possible the power and prestige as a writer he had gained with me and, instead of by means of books, to interest me face to face in Brandt himself.

Precisely because I had discovered at the last minute I was dealing with a priest, I had ruled out everything that was now taking place and which normally speaking I would be prepared for. I had still expected a hallowed atmosphere, an atmosphere of chastity, asceticism, attention and self-denying dedication of someone who in his innermost being has always continued to be a priest, with or without God.

The essay in my folder made me pig-headed and gave me the courage to postpone for the time being the arrival of an unavoidable course of events. I had been looking forward too much to a feast of the spirit to allow it, without a fight, to be perverted by life-stories into the banal game of seduction.

'But of course, of course,' Brandt said amiably when I requested him just to read my written answer to his question as to the nature of the literary text, and to give me his reaction. I bent down to take the essay from my bag and to look up the passage for him where, bold and reckless, I gave a definition of a literary text.

'Why don't you read it aloud to me yourself,' he said. Indeed, why not?

'Have you read Derrida?' he asked, when I had finished reading to him and, suddenly blushing with shyness, I looked up at him.

'No,' said I. I had indeed heard of Derrida and I had also read a thing or two about him, but I was too full of Foucault to hurl myself at the work of another, still living philosopher, and I had postponed the reading of his books time and again.

'Curious,' he said, 'most curious. What you maintain there about the essence of literature might have been written by Derrida, though he would never use the word *essence*. I can scarcely believe that you have never read a syllable of the man's work. Are you sure?'

Yes. Of course. I nodded. He'd better go on talking, for I thought this was nerve-wracking. If Derrida was a good philosopher, then Brandt was now giving me a compliment and I wanted to hear that. And yet the compliment would deprive me of all pleasure for then everything I had written had also been argued by someone else, only earlier.

'To be honest,' Brandt continued, 'I haven't been that interested in Foucault for some considerable time now. What Derrida does is a thousand times more interesting, more exciting, too, and in my opinion of a greater philosophical quality. In your piece you use Foucault to develop your thoughts further, and to distance yourself from him. You believe you end up with Nietzsche but in fact you end up with Derrida. You must read him, truly you must; you will be amazed at how much you recognise and find again of what in your definition is in fact the point, too: a better understanding of the act of writing itself. Only you are a metaphysician, to coin a phrase. You make being a writer something sacred. It reminds me of a Christian version of the definition by Plato, but then, heaven be praised, rendered tremendously banal. In your case, the author still is a bit of an absent God, a kind of hidden seducer who allows himself to be mediated for in the world by the book. Your definition also leaves me a little sad. Not only because I am a writer myself but also because, in the light of your definition, you might better not have met me in reality and that this triangular relationship between writer, book and the world should have remained purely spiritual. You are still searching passionately for the essence of things, I see, and you seek this outside of the realm of texts. To me a world outside of the text has become unthinkable.'

Clemens Brandt went and sat on the edge of the settee, and he spoke glowingly of a paper existence, an existence of which solely the word was the mysterious begetter. Now and again he would get up and fetch a book from the bookcase, read an excerpt from it to me, then, having become enthused by the quotation, to get up once more and with hurried tripping steps to bring out other books. Through reaching for the shelves, his shirt had slipped ever further from his trousers and now was hanging like a crumpled handkerchief over the top of his belt. He was losing himself so much in connecting all kinds of quotations and seeking out fine descriptions which, from Augustine to this Derrida, enjoyed kinship with one another through their dissolute paeans of praise for language, that he forgot himself completely and did not realise that he was beginning to look ever more dishevelled and boyish.

Only when there was quite a pile of books on the table and he leaned back, tired, did he discover the flap of his shirt and begin to stuff it back laboriously into his trousers. For this he had to press his back against the armrest and raise his lower torso a little. By the way in which he did this I saw that he knew no shame.

'I see I've quite undressed myself for you,' he laughed.

I was too grateful not to laugh back. He had given me

exactly what I had imagined: an inspired knowledge of the most diverse authors, different descriptions of what a literary text actually was, a view of the obsession and desire which can accompany reading and how the loneliness of this desire might still be shared with someone else. I was that other, now.

A dribbling, cheerful, shameless gnome was sitting in front of me, but now I regarded him with the gaze of someone who has just been comforted. Clemens Brandt had made something clear to me about a possible future, about a loneliness lying in store for me and which proved bearable, fertile, a kind of happiness.

I told him this, just so.

He was rather startled by the turn the conversation suddenly took, by my unexpected preparedness yet to speak about him and about how things in life would have to go on from here.

'Let's have lunch somewhere, Em,' he said.

Clemens Brandt could conceal little. When he was shaken he looked it, too.

He wore a dark-blue duffle-coat. He walked to the right of me. If I turned my face toward him and saw him from the side, I looked slap into the massive chunk of flesh that formed his torso. He walked with a springy step, on his toes. It was as if his neck was missing completely and the head had been plonked down like a fat clump of clay on top of an amorphous torso.

He had put his hands in his coat pockets. I had, too. I felt myself to be bigger than him while I wasn't. He was bigger.

Passers-by looked us over with shameless glances. By the manner in which they looked I saw how they must see us, him and me, beside one another. I was reminded of *Beauty and the Beast* while I have never seen a film of that name, or read a book which had that title. You get it from somewhere and you don't know where.

We passed over a bridge. From the opposite direction came a young couple, arm in arm, both beautiful enough to derive power from their appearance. In passing, the girl snickered too loudly and too conspicuously. She whispered something to the boy and they laughed.

Then I linked my arm with Clemens Brandt's.

We did not look at each other.

At the word 'lunch' I think of a cheese sandwich, but Clemens Brandt took me to a restaurant where a waiter in morning-dress greeted him by name, took our coats and enquired politely whether the professor would like to be seated at his usual table.

It had been clear and light outside but within the restaurant all reminiscence of the time of day was precluded. The waiter escorted us to a table in a corner and lit a candle. This being submerged in timelessness made me calm and contented. A case of come what may, again. I felt inclined to slouch in my chair and close my eyes the way I frequently do when I am sitting beside someone in the car in the dark. For, then I have it irrevocably, this languid feeling of happiness and relaxation, the feeling of having been snatched away from time, and because of this I am indifferent to the hour of my death and firmly prepared to die there and then, if necessary.

'Do you like it here?' he asks.

'Yes, very much,' I say and I regret that my willingness to oblige has to be accompanied by the change in tone from the courteously formal to the familiar.

'Life is beautiful,' sighs Brandt. 'I am glad I wrote back to you and that you're here now. It *is* an unexpected encounter, don't you think?'

Yes, I think so too.

He eats there almost daily, mainly on his own, occasionally with a student and always between one and three in the afternoon. In the morning he has oatmeal porridge, in the evening a cup of soup. Three hot meals a day is a relic from the monastery, one of the few.

'Not counting this,' he said, rubbing his hand over his tonsure and then pushing a strand of hair that had dropped forwards back behind his ear, 'but that's a remnant of a different order, less voluntary.'

Because I enquire after this, he tells what happens, entering a monastery, putting on a habit, the shaving of the pate.

'Viewed properly, it's a kind of disfigurement,' he says, 'the branding of a herd animal so that an ineradicable trace remains by which everyone can distinguish to whom or what you belong. To be in the service of the sacred means to be set apart, to be separated from the society of mankind. I was also reminded of this when you were reading your piece to me. When you enter a monastery, the idea is that you sever all connections with which you are attached to your previous life. You are put into perfect isolation, are given a new name, new clothes, you learn another language, eat different food and you run roughshod over the body. You kill your old personality in order to be resurrected a new man. It's all very pagan, really, some archaic initiation rites with a fixed sequence of stadia.'

'Did you have a vocation?' I ask quickly, for fear that he is about to undermine and end his story.

'I thought so at the time,' he replies thoughtfully, 'at the time I did. Later on, I went and studied psychology and I now believe more to have answered the call of my own mother than anything else. I must have felt that it was her dearest wish to have a sacred child. And I didn't mind becoming that child to her. Hm, quite. For Her and not for

105

Him. D'you think that odd?'

Not I. I shake my head and smile at him in encouragement to continue.

'I recall most vividly indeed the fantasy about how I, personally, would set out to render void the story of the Fall of Man, how I would turn back time and rid the world of the story once and for all. I felt dreadfully sorry for God, I thought. God had had the best of intentions with us. He had neatly arranged paradise for us: only the very best, scrimped on nothing. Our lives were protected, safe, secure. There need not be a single word spoken in anger between people, no pain need be endured, nothing awaited us of which we need be afraid. We need not be chased and haunted by anything and we never need doubt because we could simply follow the paths God had set out for us and do things the way they had been intended by Him – and He meant well.

'And then Eve allows herself to be tempted by the devil and she eats of that tree of Knowledge. Gruesome! I imagined it all, how God saw it happen before His own eyes and had to look on powerlessly how His own creatures hurled themselves into the void and to their doom. It was an unbearable thought, but I now suspect myself of rather having relished this fantasy very much indeed, looking back. I could not recall the story of the Fall of Man often enough. Then, when I had reached the scene where Eve's hesitating beside the tree, I could have shouted out loud with fear: "Don't do it! Please, don't do it!" But she did. She did it each time again. And poor old God had to witness it again each time, too. I'd be moved to tears, then.'

He looks up. The story has turned him melancholy.

Me too.

'The curious thing was, I had no grip on that fantasy. Every attempt to intervene, to bend the course of events

106

and to assume a splendid, heroic role myself, by strangling the snake with bare hands or dashing off to God on the trot to warn Him in time, provoked only a feeling of paralysis. I couldn't do anything to my fantasy. I had to let the story run its course the same way, time and again.'

'You weren't outside it. You're in it yourself.'

'Right,' he says, 'but in whom?'

Tensely, he sounds my face. He's afraid of what I am going to say, of a coinciding of the reply he gives himself each time and mine. I know the answer but I cannot give it to him, I cannot bear to.

'God or devil,' I say as airily as possible, 'it's all the same to me.'

Then the waiter sets down two steaming plates in front of our noses.

Clemens Brandt hovers, bent forward, above his sliced suckling pig and stuffs the first few mouthfuls in at great speed, too much in one go. His elbows are pushed outward, stretched out like two clipped wings. His head sits sunk between his shoulders and somewhere behind his ear looms the contour of his hump. Without laying down his fork and wiping his lips, gleaming with grease, on the damask serviette, he grabs, maintaining the same posture, for his glass of wine and washes the food down in firm gulps. He only raises his eyes occasionally in order to look at the lamb chop on my plate.

I regard him with mounting amazement. He believes himself to be perfectly unobserved. It is either stupidity or innocence, and I swing backwards and forwards between revulsion and being moved. I try to remember how nervous and excited I was before I got to know him, what the name Clemens Brandt evoked in me before I was sitting here opposite him. This makes the day somewhat less real again, and the mixture of revulsion, curiosity and pity the more so.

My stomach reacts, startled by the unusual hour at which it is having to cope with dishes of eventide. I eat slowly. I'm afraid of rumbling noises burbling up. Because Clemens keeps silent, I tell him how as a child I went over to the parish priest and asked him how I might become a priest. As I am recounting this I look at him, at his moving jaws, his lips, his hands, his face. The story doesn't touch him and this is why I make it even wilder than it was. His face betrays not a single reaction. Discouraged by his unwillingness, I bring it to an end quickly, afraid to bore him even further.

When Clemens Brandt leans back and rubs his pear-shaped tummy elaborately, I have still barely eaten anything of my lamb chop. His eyes roam time and again towards the straight bone with the succulent meat. I suddenly feel awkward and expect at any moment to see his hand shooting across the table to snatch the chop from my plate and him then starting to gnaw away at it ostentatiously.

He contains himself.

'Why does this interest you so much?' he asks, when I have put down my knife and fork.

'Why does what?'

'Priests, God, ordination and the like,' he says.

Questions by others mostly put me on the spot. They sound as if I have never posed them to myself and the more they seem unknown to me, the more weight they have. There must be a reason, mustn't there, why you have never asked yourself the questions you evoke in somebody else? Is there something you keep a secret from yourself, a hidden evil, an undesirable trait of character, an unknown domain within yourself of which the other, the one putting the question, has gained an inkling? I like it all right, but I prefer to take them home with me, to the place where I am alone and only then can truly think of a reply. The answer I give on the spot is improvised, incomplete, a first stab at a guess.

'I'm not sure I know,' I say. 'Perhaps because it's something so absolute, becoming a priest. After all, it's no ordinary profession with which you earn your daily bread in everyday life and beside which you live yet another life, in your spare time. Surely it encompasses your entire life, I think. Your life coincides with your work, with what you have become, I mean. I can't put it properly. In my view, it's absolute dedication, something all-encompassing and through this also elevated, rather. Indeed. The same applies to being an artist, I think. It is to be compared with it. That, too, is a choice for a way of life.'

'And what am I, in your view,' he asks, 'the artist or the priest?'

'The priest,' I say at once, even though I know that I disappoint him with this. 'To me you are the priest, I don't know why, for you don't look like any priest I know and moreover the image I had of a priest doesn't agree in any way with the manner in which I have got to know you now. And yet you *are* the priest.'

My answer has not succeeded in wiping the despondency from his face, so I add that he is much more sensuous, earthier, more normal, a hedonist.

He smiles.

'You may be right, perhaps,' he says, quietly, 'but I don't feel myself to be a priest any more. By now, it's all so far behind me, after all. It's the first time in years that I talk about it with someone again. You stir me into talking about it, about the priesthood, God. I don't know why I never get round to it any more of my own accord, even to think about it or to remember those days. I probably still do the same thing – perhaps that's why. To be a priest is really a kind of being cult-licensed and just like the monastery or the church, university is a cult-community, with rituals, initiations, trials, with masters and pupils. I still practise the service of the word.'

'Do you find it unpleasant to talk about it?'

'No, no,' he says reassuringly, 'it only leaves me with some confusing feelings. On the one hand, it's very pleasant and I have the feeling of talking with you about something essential, but on the other hand the unpleasant sensation creeps up on me of deceiving you a little by speaking of something of which I am no longer convinced and perhaps never have been, for that matter. God: God seems like a theory which in the past I adhered to and have rejected as barren later on. For so long, to me, God has been ousted from his place by other words with a capital letter. I distrust myself when I speak of it. I think I only still use his name in order to fascinate you with my story.'

His voice sounds like that of a condemned man who confesses his guilt and asks the other whether he should show even more contrition. Again it strikes me that his eyes sometimes do not co-operate with the sound of his voice. In the main, his eyes are as they are now: challenging, provocative, recalcitrant.

I continue to rely on the voice.

I bend forward and for a moment I put my hand on his.

'Don't upset yourself,' I say, 'that's what stories are for, aren't they?'

'For what?'

'To fascinate.'

It's coming up for five when he accompanies me to the station. I lean heavily on his arm because I am tiddly from the wine. Outside the restaurant, the world suddenly has too much reality to be wanted to be seen by me like that. I squeeze my eyes half-shut and allow myself to be led like one blind.

110

On Tuesday, there's an artistic postcard. The handwriting is tiny but perfectly legible. What's put there does not surprise me. The following day the post at an early hour delivers a parcel of books by Jacques Derrida. A letter's enclosed.

Writing back takes me hours. We really ought to leave it at this. I feel an indefinable fear of all that is about to occur and I dare not seek an explanation for it. Time and again, I re-read his letter. Thought of you all the time, deeply impressed, a touch confused, next week, America, away a month, meet before then, weekend, talk together, have dinner, possibly stay the night?

He's Clemens Brandt, isn't he? He trusts me, he knows much, it is an honour to mean something to him.

In the end, I write back to him that much of what he said continues to haunt me, his tales about the monastery and the priesthood inspire me in the writing of my Master's thesis and seem to make something clear to me about my own life as well, though I do not yet know precisely what and how; that of course I, too, wish to see him again, gladly, and that then we could discuss this, that I'm delighted with the books, thanks, that he's welcome in Amsterdam and staying the night no problem.

I myself have everything under control, haven't I? Well?

When, on Saturday afternoon, Clemens Brandt steps into my room, face beaming, clumsily holds out a big bunch of flowers to me and presses a bungled, wet kiss on my cheeks, I have everything under control but myself.

He is wearing a brand-new, light-weight suit, too frivolous for the time of year, too pallid beside the colour of his skin and so thin his hump seems once as big again. He has bought it specially for today. He feels a different man, exuberant, happy, young.

It hurts me. I'm going too far. Even his eyes are a little

watery today. Poor gnome, dotty desire.

'D'you like it?' he asks without doubting my answer.

'Yes,' say I. 'I think it's fine, Clemens.'

'Suits me?'

'Perfectly.'

'How are you? You look rather tense.'

So I am. With regret and remorse, I see his face cloud over, his excitement shrink, see the dreams of the last few days, the insanity of the purchase of the suit, the lonely pleasure in sending the post, the adolescent tension during the drive from Groningen to Amsterdam, disappear from his eyes. To get in ahead of the instant when the loss of an imagined love is complete and he, utterly sobered, must discover himself in a ramshackle house in Amsterdam, dressed like a circus monkey, like a fool with ridiculous figments of the imagination, I hurriedly say it's caused by the unusual nature of our getting to know one another, being so quickly at ease with someone.

That I like him very much, is what I say.

That I'm afraid to disappoint him.

That I'm afraid I will hurt him.

That I trust him.

That it'll pass, in no time, now that he's here.

I gabble the tears into my eyes.

'Em-darling, really,' he says and he comes and stands close to me. 'You're very sweet. You needn't be afraid. All's fine, nothing's expected from you.'

'D'you mean that?'

'From the bottom of my heart,' he says. 'If you wish to receive what I have to give, you make me perfectly happy.'

These are liberating words, they relieve me. In gratitude I rest my head on his shoulder a moment.

May he take his delusions out on me, then.

By nightfall we walked to Bickerseiland. Clemens had

112

reserved a table at the *Gouden Reael* and requested a place at the window specially, he said, so we could stare across the IJ. It was the last day of March and still too chilly to be outside without an overcoat in the evening, but Clemens maintained not to find it cold in the slightest and had left his coat behind in the car. He had linked his arm in mine and hopped along beside me just like a big, white pigeon who has puffed up the feathers round its neck and has let its head sink into the down. I noticed that he turned his head toward me now and then, but I didn't look back. We had talked much already and this was the time to be silent. I thought about whether it added up what he had said to me, that I was an old-fashioned platonist and still stubbornly believed in the true, in something real outside the false and that I was in search of this.

'You don't turn a hair at words such as soul, truth, the essence, good and evil,' he had said. And this is true.

I go on about the soul, sin, good and God as if there's nothing to it at all. Even now, though they no longer stand for what they once represented: the soul as a little cloth, somewhere in the vicinity of the heart, which shows up a dirty mark the moment you lie, cheat, curse, carp, steal or even if you only fantasise about doing all of these. It only gets cleansed when you honestly confess your sins to the parish priest for he has something you don't: a direct line to the great, grey man in heaven.

My image of the soul altered a little when a new toy came on to the market, a writing pad with a slide-mechanism. With a pointed marker without ink you would write something on the plastic surface and when you then pulled the slide, the words were erased. The soul was something like that, I thought. When the priest asked for it, God pulled the slide of my soul and erased my verbal sins (lied seventeen times to almost everybody, carped daily at my brothers, one theft of chewing gum at the Spar,

113

feign remorse after punishment by Miss) at a stroke.

One day, the soul was a thing, sin an erasable word, and God a man no longer. Without an accompanying image I have continued to be attached to the words themselves. These are the stubborn metaphors from the very first stories that reached my ears. They form the topography of my primaeval story in which the great questions of life and death happened to have acquired this shape and no other.

I do not avoid them.

I can't see the point of replacing them by other words which boil down to the same thing anyway.

'Everything is a grotesque, theatrical performance, it is, in the end,' Clemens had said with a deep but satisfied sigh. Sigh or no sigh, Brandt or no Brandt, I thought it a hogwash philosophy. In my head I prepared myself to provide him, in an effective manner, quietly but sparing nothing, with the incontrovertible evidence of the inanity of this thought.

'*Everything* is an empty word, for nothing is said by it. Its use is evidence of a certain kind of stupidity. It glosses over our ignorance of why we are here and what we are to do with life. You call me an old-fashioned platonist because I angle for the soul, but your idea stems from long before Plato still. With your "Everything is theatre" you may number yourself with Heraclitus and his chums, for whom the whole thing was taken care of, too, when they dreamed up that everything was water, fire or air. Not being able to distinguish anything is what it is ...'

I was jolted from my ponderings when someone loudly let 'Theresa' skim like a shard across the water.

Daniel was standing on one of the landing stages at the quayside. He walked towards us and suddenly I became painfully aware of the man on my arm. This was

114

generously recompensed by Daniel's surprised look when I introduced them and again had the pleasant sensation of the names of Clemens Brandt crossing each other, names of which one belonged to the ugly hunchback and the other on the spine of a book.

To Daniel's question as to whether he was the author, Clemens reacted surlily, not at all in the friendly tone of voice I was used to from him. It made the interest he had in me suddenly special again. I knew Daniel Daalmeyer's harum-scarum relish for speaking but, because I had the feeling of having to take him into my protection against Clemens's attitude of fending him off, I enquired after the reason for his absence from university.

'I'm writing a book,' Daniel said, startling me. He turned to me completely and reminded me with agile tongue of the comparison he made at the time between Hegel's scheme of life and the biography of a sufferer.

'Then it suddenly came to me, and that's what my book is now about. I started on it immediately. It's going to be a work of genius, a mixture of autobiography, philosophy and a medical treatise. In fact you're really standing at the cradle of a masterpiece,' he said, chortling.

My arm is a good conductor for the growing unrest of Clemens. When I see from the corner of my eye how he raises his free hand and ostentatiously scratches the top of his head, I let Daniel know I'll be ringing him soon and wish him luck with the writing.

'And who was that, pray?' asks Clemens when we walk on.

'The epileptic,' say I.

'That you can be so impossible, too,' I said with undisguised admiration to Clemens as I looked up, having indeed stared across the IJ from behind the window.

'Was I really impossible? I'm wont to be like that, rather

indifferent, I should say. I have also needed an entire lifetime to acquire the feeling of not needing anyone any more. That's why you are so dangerous for me, too,' he added.

Apparently I was looking not a little fearful, for then he tried to take away any threat.

'You come as a gift from heaven, mind, honestly, and I am enjoying this like I haven't enjoyed things for ages, even my own confusion. Perhaps you can only be truly open to people when you finally acquiesce to being yourself, with all your own quirks. I have learned to desire only that which is dependent on my own actions, which I have a grip on myself and which I do not need to receive from outside or above or from whom or whatever it may be. It's a matter of sharply separating two worlds, the world of dreams and that of reality, of day and of night, of private and public, if you will.

'Now that I've got to know you, a kind of breach is being forced in my neatly erected partition wall and then things run into one another a little again. Never mind, though.'

Clemens had spoken to me in a serious, mild tone of voice but didn't succeed in taking away my unrest. We were handed a menu. Reading and choosing from it was made difficult for me by a strange premonition, the suspicion that Clemens wanted to tell me a secret, one he had prepared himself for and which he needed to unburden himself of before leaving for America. He was summoning up his courage. Revealing the secret was an attempt to cut a clear path for us and I fretted about whether I ought to secure my own equanimity of spirit by adjusting the course of his fantasies about us, or ought I to give in to his desire to emerge from hidden shelter, and thus also to my pride in being taken into his confidence.

We ordered extensively.

116

I needn't worry my head about the night, not for the time being, in any case.

'I don't understand it, what you're saying. You live pretty publicly, don't you? What does your life of the night look like then?' I try to look like someone who won't take to his heels in the face of any answer, nothing human is alien to me, seen it all before, no fool like a damn fool, won't bite your head off: that look.

'I don't really know whether I want to talk about it,' Clemens says hesitantly. He fathoms my gaze but immediately casts down his eyes again.

'Women,' say I.

'Prostitutes,' says he.

In hindsight I'd say that it wasn't the word nor his voice, but his eyes were the ones that made me go cold and my midriff tightened, tensed. He didn't look timid, furtive or shy; he looked gleefully gluttonous. But he wasn't looking gluttonous at the thought of whores, he was looking at me. My reaction was his pleasure.

I saw it as a challenge. (Wrong.)

I asked on. (Wrong.)

'Whores?' I say when the waiter sets down the sweet-meat in front of me.

'Not ordinary ones,' Clemens says when the waiter has absented himself.

Then he gets the reaction which he is waiting for: I don't know any more. I know nothing yet of perversions then.

Clemens registers assiduously my sudden fear. It renders him mild and careful.

'Enjoying yours, Em?'

'Yes, it's delicious.'

'Might I taste a bit?'

'Of course. No, wait. I'll cut you a little piece myself.' They come to his place once a month. The lady, Justine, acts on his behalf. She selects them for him. He, too, knows that this is not her real name, but he thinks often of Justine. He has never seen her, knows her only from the telephone conversations and he has become attached to her. He thinks she lovingly selects the girls for him. Occasionally, he catches himself at thinking of her when he is with one of the women.

She only has special women. Special women bring along a suitcase. It takes quite a number of things or else it won't work.

They shackle him, hang him up, tie him down, beat him, tear him apart.

'It's terrible,' he says. When he brings the wine-glass to his mouth, his hand trembles. He takes a draught, chokes and has a terrific coughing fit. Barking, he apologises, begs leave and walks to the toilet. He trips but manages to keep his footing.

I watch him go but I'm no longer there.

When I pull the shirt from his trousers he groans.

'No, oh no.'

Slowly, I unbutton the shirt. He puts his hands on my hips but I take them away.

'No, Clemens, don't touch me.'

Nor do I want kisses.

I take the glasses from his nose, pull the shirt down along his arms and slip the undervest over his head. He has many big birthmarks on his chest, warts almost, with little hairs. Only the skin surrounding his hump is perfect. I caress it. I kiss his nipples. He groans.

I kneel down in front of him and undo the laces of his shoes, set him down on the edge of the bed and take off his shoes and then his socks. One by one, I take his feet into my hands, rub the instep, knead the soles, slip my tongue between his toes, lick his feet clean.

118

He puts a hand on my head. I take it away and put it back in his lap.

Still knelt down, I loosen his trouser-belt and simultaneously take down his trousers and underpants. He is sitting hunched on the bed and is following all my movements. When I get up and bend forwards to draw back the sheets, I hear him sobbing quietly. I look him in the face.

'This is the happiest day of my life,' he says.

I say nothing at all. I grasp him by his shoulders, swivel him sideways and pull up the sheets over him.

I only run into myself again when, without any discernible cause, I wake up in the middle of the night. I am lying on my back and stare at the ceiling. It is Sunday.

I concentrate on the grating sound of his breathing, imagining with accuracy a windpipe the while, a plug of slime in it being driven upwards when he breathes out and just not managing it as it slips screechingly back down the sides of his windpipe, bumps on to the bottom, up again, down.

It's no good.

I am perfectly unreachable, except by disgust.

Chapter V

THE PHYSICIST

We bury Miel van Eysden one morning in January. The weather does its utmost. The wind could hardly be more piercing. It chases some black thunder-clouds above our heads, now scattering them widely then driving them back together again. Occasionally some icy-cold rain gushes down from one of the clouds and lands exactly on the small procession of strangers, chilled to the bone, who walk behind the bier. And that's the way it should be, too.

Miel's mother walks at the head of the procession, immediately behind the hearse. Her big nose is bright red, the white hair is matted and looks like a straw wig. She resembles a clown. She walks alone and proud. She stares at the ground. At times she has to hold back her pace as otherwise she will walk past the black car altogether. She does not need to be supported by anyone.

From time to time I look at the man beside me. Not too often. When I look at him, I don't know for the first few minutes how to calm myself and silence my jubilant tummy.

I try to think of Miel and of death but my head spins a bit because of this, and I think of death, love and life, all at the same time. The best case I am able to imagine, is that Miel himself is still at the root of this, is directing things in such

120

a way that his death is the point of origin again of other entanglements, and still serves some purpose, at least.

I do calculations in my head. The figures belonging to this day, to this month and year, I add up, multiply, subtract, divide. They won't come to thirty-three. How many days ago did I receive that letter? What date was it then?

The rattle of the letterbox was always a signal to me to stop whatever I was doing. It was no rare occurrence for me to stop reading, mid-sentence, and rush down the stairs to pick up the post.

A number of envelopes were lying on the hallway floor. From the top of the final staircase I could survey the square metre floor-surface and already try to estimate whether there was something interesting among them, and whether I was not being fobbed-off with disappointingly grey-green girobank-envelopes. Letters were best and I was in luck that day for I saw at once a blue, air-mail envelope, that queen among envelopes.

Once downstairs, I saw that the letter was addressed to M. Lune, which surprised me for the handwriting on the envelope was not that of the astrologer. There was no sender's name indicated on the back.

Post causes a strange kind of tension and I am addicted to tension. It's a curious hankering as the tension to which you are addicted is accompanied by an equally fierce longing to eradicate it as soon as possible, thus putting paid to the pleasure.

With letters you are able to divide up the game nicely and you have the whole field to yourself. A wrapped-up story lies there and its course is unknown. You can be umpire between the tension concerning the unread contents of the letter and the desire to learn them as quickly as possible. That which once was written and sent, is within easy reach. No one can take that away from you again.

I put down the envelope on the table, unopened, as is my wont with letters. I went into the kitchen. In as controlled a manner as was possible I buttered a slice of brown bread, looked in the refrigerator for something to put on it, but discovered I had run clean out of cheese. Things were turning awkward. I could stretch matters by going to the cheesemonger's round the corner, go the whole hog and prepare an omelette with fresh garden herbs, or limit myself to cucumber which was to hand. I plumped for the last. One-nil to the letter. I made a little more of a fuss about the cucumber, sliced it thinly, sprinkled it with pepper, salt and oregano and then I suddenly recalled that I still had some ground horseradish. I anointed the plate with a touch of this, alongside the slice of bread. In the room, I cleared a corner of the table, walked back another time to the kitchen to fetch a glass and the plate, returned and poured myself some red wine from the already opened bottle there. The score was one-all. I took a draught of wine, to life and to the loneliness of happiness, and I opened the crackling envelope with a blade of a pair of scissors.

There were two sheets inside the envelope, a blue one written by hand and something which at first sight looked like a telex or a computer print-out. On both the front and back of the latter sheet had been written, in unfamiliar handwriting:

'Better read this first.'

To keep up the tension I controlled myself, did not look at the reverse of the blue sheet to see who was the author but heeded the instruction and first read the sheet that was typed.

AUVERS-SUR-OISE – Tracker dogs yesterday evening discovered the mortal remains of the 47-year-old M. van

E. from Amsterdam. The man had already been missing for a week. He had fallen into a twenty-metre deep chasm. According to the *gendarmerie*, going by the head-wounds he sustained, he must have died instantly.

I stared at the notice and tried to let it penetrate that this was about the astrologer, that he was dead. This took a moment. But then I knew. Sorrow would have to come quickly now, in my view, but it was stuck behind a square block that stabbed my windpipe with its sharp corners. Only when, unasked for, some very old sentences occurred to me, ready-made, as if they had always lain waiting patiently inside my head in order to be repeated at all times and endlessly, did I gain enough space for air and for the pain as well.

'God rest his soul,' I murmured, 'the Lord have mercy on him, may he rest in peace, *ad resurrectionem mortuorum.*'

My poor friend, poor soul.

The blue sheet was already nothing like as exciting any more. I suspected by whom it had been written.

Paris, January 1984

Dear M. Lune,

Forgive me for having to address you with a name which perhaps now hurts you, but I have never heard Miel speak of you other than as Monsieur Lune. And I actually do think it rather beautiful. I don't know your real name and in Miel's diary you are down as this. Just like Miel, that.

Enclosed announcement will be printed in the Dutch newspapers today or tomorrow. I believe you have the right to be appraised of Miel's death in a more personal manner than that.

Mrs van Eysden was approached direct by the French

police and identified Miel the morning after the discovery of the body. She rang me from Auvers. She said something about a peaceful smile round his mouth. To comfort me, I think.

All being well, his body will be flown over to the Netherlands and he will be buried in Hengelo Monday next. The Van Eysdens have a family vault there. His father lies there already.

Tomorrow morning I will take the train to Holland and will then attend the funeral on Monday. I should very much like to meet you. Miel often talked about you. Upon my arrival I'll give you a call to find out whether a meeting would suit you and whether we can arrange something.

Do take care, for it's all very sad indeed. My apologies for the awful scrawl.

Hugo Morland

The astrologer would always begin and end his travels through France in Paris. His favourite lodgings were with Hugo Morland and his wife Sybille. He was a Dutchman, she was French and both worked as physicists at the *Institut d'Astrophysique*.

The astrologer had once designated them as being the mirror image of his own parents: all that turned out negative in them returned in the reverse, positive form in the Morlands. How the astrologer had got to know Hugo Morland, I no longer remembered, but I knew that this was a friendship of years' standing which had commenced in his youth in Holland.

The astrologer's stories had always made me curious as to Monsieur and Madame Curie, as he was also wont to call them. When, a few years ago, I visited Paris together with him it was a great disappointment to discover that the

Morlands were off to a conference in Berkeley for the same period.

I am secretly in awe of physics. If a place can still be found anywhere for the image of the absent-minded, formula-juggling inventor of genius it would have to be in physics. Compared with such an exact science, philosophy quickly pales into airy-fairiness which in no way can keep up with what physicists have to report on identical problems to those which philosophers worry their heads about. The origins of the universe, the origins of life, the limits of the world, the essence of time, and then to discover the internal connections between them so that all is encapsulated in a single, simple, all-encompassing idea, that is the point of it all, isn't it? So what *are* all these ill-tempered goings-on between humanities and sciences?

I also tend to ascribe a clear mind to them, these physicists, more hygienic than those of philosophers, devoid of romanticism but, because of this – how to put it – also rather non-literary. His desperate attempts to be a creature of reality notwithstanding, the philosopher remains a slave of a spurned form of rhetoric.

The pain of remembering the astrologer, our hours, our conversations together, his sad, sorry eyes, the curved, bent body, his tears and his oddity, was being thwarted by the exciting prospect of at last meeting with a real physicist and man-of-science. By going back and forth between us, the astrologer had mutually connected us by a web of tales and I was curious to see whether his descriptions were accurate. I also wouldn't mind knowing why a physicist had advised the astrologer at the time to take back Foucault for me.

It was Thursday, four days prior to the funeral taking place. He rang that same evening.

125

'Monsieur Lune? Yes, Morland speaking,' he said and then was perfectly silent.

I believe I felt it immediately, a tremor, caused by the slowness with which he enunciated his name, the pulsating rhythm in which the words came through, each word marked out, surrounded by silence and rocking in peace. The silence afterwards was so utterly complete that it provoked a tension which I had to rend asunder by welcoming him elaborately, had a good journey, etc.

Each answer he gave was minimal and had the same rhythm as his first words, with that brazenly long interval in between.

He wanted to have some fish. We would meet in the lobby of his hotel and then have dinner at Lucius's.

'How will we recognise each other?'

'We will, all right,' he said.

Too true.

He was standing, his arms crossed, leant relaxedly against a marble column in the centre of the lobby. The slowness of his utterance had found its graphic continuation in the markings of his facial features. In his face the deeply sunk, half-hooded eyes were particularly noteworthy. He was forty or thereabouts, had a balding head, a broad face and a large mouth whose lower lip rested upon a sloping, prominent chin without being sharply differentiated from it. His upper lip was different, narrower and parted in the middle by an elongated line like a swallow's tail.

He was not a decidedly handsome man. He had something I had never discovered in anyone else before. I first heard it in the rhythm of his speech, then saw it in his face and later on in all the movements of his body: a lazy springiness, the sensuality of a tempo. When he walked he had something of a sated, lazy lion beneath a scorching sun. No gesture of his was brusque or abrupt.

He looked at me but didn't stir. He didn't smile, didn't raise his eyebrows, put nothing in place, at the ready, in that face, in order to be able to play out the game of greeting on first encounter in the usual way. It confused me utterly. I thought him irresistible.

'Hugo?' I ask, as I walk up to him.

'Lune,' he says and slowly detaches himself from the column.

We wait for the monkfish. 'Was it really an accident?' we have wondered. We don't know.

Three months prior to his death, Hugo saw him in Paris still.

'He was already very chaotic when he arrived from Amsterdam and you last saw him. Afterwards, he roamed through the South a bit, again seeking a spot, I think. It must have been late September. He rang us and asked whether he could stay with us for a few nights.

'He looked very wild and bushy, worse than ever before. I could barely follow what he was saying. Miel had become the sole initiate into his own system. All those connections, it really was too much. At that time he spoke often of his aversion to Van Gogh and yet he was implacably sucked towards the places where Van Gogh had lived and worked. "And then I'd suddenly be standing in Arles again", you know how Miel could put such things. He'd done some walking about the place there, he told us, across the fields, without actually knowing what he was looking for. Suddenly a crow had run amok, or something like, and had attacked him. It had pecked his ear and then flown away again. He had been very upset by this.

'Miel frequently would also tell strange tales. I've always believed them. He was no fantasist, when he was talking about true reality, at least. And he even showed it to me, the scab of a wound to his ear. Odd, huh? Nevertheless, that was the first time I thought Miel was turning stark raving mad. No, that wasn't it, really. I believe that Miel himself for the first time in his life thought that he was going mad.'

'Poor astrologer.'

'*Le besoin de la fatalité*, Sybille called it.'

'Nicely put,' I said and babbled on a bit about the comfort in a fitting expression, the poetic description, the apt image. To no avail. The image of the lonely astrologer, roaming the fields of France, and the choking desire to press myself up against Hugo's body, to weep there long and loudly, were not so easily set to flight.

As the evening progressed, and the life-story of the astrologer became more complete than it had ever been to me previously, my feeling of regret mounted. Repeatedly, painful moments occurred to me: when I had been sharp with him or hadn't wanted to let him in.

The astrologer had been the older boy-next-door to Hugo. They had the same hobby: the stars. At eleven, Hugo was given a telescope by his parents and from that time onward, the astrologer would spend entire days with him, in Hugo's attic. The astrologer didn't like being at home. Hugo thought it unpleasant there, too. He described the old Van Eysden as being a gruff, authoritarian man, a good scientist, a poor father, in love with his wife's accuracy, the unplumbable depths of the earth and of his own intellect, and full of a chill indifference to anything not included in these. Miel was not included. He had been terrified of his father.

'Miel did always have the idea of having been mutilated for life by his parents. He never managed to get rid of that. In fact, he always did remain a very childlike man, frightened to undertake something himself, frightened to

128

fail in the eyes of his father. His mother ought to have rescued him but his mother worshipped that man. She always did idolise her husband.

'At times Miel would enter my room trembling with suppressed rage, such that I thought he'd explode before my very eyes. "Bash him on the nose then," I'd say to him but this he couldn't do. And so we'd then take a bit of a look at the stars again. This would calm him down. Then, according to him, he'd be able to see it all and understand. "It has to be," he would say, almost happy. He'd have seen that his father's Mars was blocking his Sun that day, or some such. All that tosh kept him going.'

We laugh at one other, wistfully. I do not dare tell him that I would like nothing better than for the astrologer to be sitting here with us at the table and reading the stars of both of us. This is why I tell him what I'm forced to think about all the time, of the image of the wheel in the astrologer's head and how it now has been crushed, together with his brains.

'True,' Hugo said, 'he had the heavens in his head, always. What he did was to a certain extent the same as what I do. He worked with precise measurements, knew what it looked like up above, watched, calculated, ascertained the positions of the planets in space, right down to the last degree, knew their orbits. Only then he turned magician and I didn't. The moment he had charted the heavens, he began to use the topology of heaven to map a landscape of the human spirit. That's where the mystification starts, of course. The magician doesn't stick with the stars themselves but jumps from the top down, the calculations in his hand, and then begins to hold forth, asserting something about people's characters and how this is connected with the stars. An astronomer, too, seeks connections, but *he* stays up there, with the stars themselves, and tries to find something out, if you can put it like that, about their behaviour.'

Could he understand this: why the one became an astrologer and the other an astronomer?

'I have read some time or other that the philosophy you espouse in the end has something to do with whom you are, as a person. Is that so?'

I nod.

'We were different individuals, he and I. You could say that Miel had a need for a personal fate, but you might just as well say that this was a need for a figure of authority, for someone who laid the law down for him, approved or disapproved of him – judged him, in any case. I believe I've become a physicist because I will not bear any form of authority. It's the boyhood dream of the physicist, to overturn the existing, authoritative laws. Physics legitimise never viewing something as absolute or sacrosanct, and such an attitude suits me. I have made it my profession.'

We ate little and drank much.

'You're in luck,' said Hugo when we were standing outside at almost ten. He had put a hand on my shoulder and had cast a glance upward. I understood he meant the full moon, hovering, perfectly round, above Amsterdam.

'It remains a curious idea,' he said. 'You see those stars and you're looking at something that no longer exists. What you see now is time past.'

I knew that. I had read it somewhere.

The hand on my shoulder weighed more heavily than that knowledge.

We walked back to his hotel. He wanted to get to bed in good time, he'd said. The journey had tired him and he had promised Sybille he'd ring.

The disappointment hurt too much already and I

130

resolved not to give myself any ideas – which didn't work.

After we had taken leave in front of the entrance to the hotel, when he had taken my head in his hands, pressed a kiss on my mouth, calm, unhurried, without clumsy angularity, and had said that Miel couldn't have thought up a better name, I managed to keep cycling until I knew for sure that I was obscured from his view, and then I dismounted and, hanging over the railing of a bridge, let a screeching bout of crying come over me, as muffled as possible.

'Bastard,' I cursed the night because I didn't know anyone else it was intended for and, moreover, because I think that you should never say something like that out loud to anyone in particular.

So what do I have to offer? Nothing. Compared with him, I'm a scared bundle of nerves and he is of course perfectly contented with his Frenchwoman. There's no out-gunning that. Frenchwoman: more or less the equivalent of perfection. A beautiful woman and master-lover, svelte, slender, long-legged, self-assured, elegant, refined, sophisticated, and she's intelligent as well. They work together so what more do you want? *M. and Mme. Curie*, not since Plato has perfect harmony between a man and a woman been represented so acutely as by the name of this married couple. He loves her. He's always going on about her, Sybille. He is splendid. This is absurd, stupid desire.

A ringing telephone puts an end to my monologue.

'Lune,' he says, 'I want to see the sea. From two onwards I have a car at my disposal. Coming?'

Rambles along the beach are nothing for me. I'm bored at the seaside. It's icy outside. In no time I'm petrified. I have to wear flat walking shoes: then he really *will* be twice as tall. The wind gives me a head like a beetroot. He's married.

131

'Yes.'

The car was well-heated and he drove unabashedly slowly. With his left lower-arm, he leant on the door handle and his right hand lay on top of the steering wheel. All other cars passed us. It didn't bother him. I couldn't care less, either. He was silent and looked at the landscape a bit, and occasionally at me. I, too, had nothing to say and looked a lot at him.

I trusted him. The strange thing about Hugo was that his trustworthiness was precisely instilled by the unpredictability of his reactions, by a lack of theatre. All that mug-bending of convention had no effect on him whatsoever and even became in my own eyes, because of his calm refusal to answer a smile with a smile, a nod with a nod, a glance with a glance, an empty play of grimaces. But you are used to it, aren't you, for someone else to come up to you and, like an actor to a prompt from his fellow, react immediately to you, pulling his own face in the preordained creases, and not to leave you behind in the chill loneliness of an unreciprocated gesture. This is precisely what Hugo did do. It sent me every time into a giggly mood: a little nervous, ridiculously alone, and at the same time full of admiration for his unusual manner of toppling an expected causality.

After ten minutes' walk I was chilled to the bone, he could see it. We walked at once to a restaurant in the dunes and it took too long for my taste even so, before we made it there.

'Rotten circulation,' he muttered when I brought out ten frightfully white fingers from my gloves. He took my hands in his warm ones and held them quietly. I looked at him and smiled. He looked at me, too, and did not smile, that is.

Again I was surprised about those eyes of Hugo's.

Yesterday it might have been fatigue, a sleepy look, but today they were the same still, sunk behind high vaulted, half-hooded eyelids.

A waiter came to take our order and I thought we'd been like this long enough and took the opportunity of drawing back my hands towards me. Before letting them go, he strengthened his grip a moment. This confused me. My hands were suddenly a burden to me: they would have been much better placed there, with him.

We took coffee and brandy and I asked him what precisely he did, back there in Paris.

'Doing sums.'

'So what do you calculate?' I asked, and then he tried to explain to me what it means to calculate probabilities, why in physics the issue was no longer matter, but tendencies, events, why he had to work with such a thing as probability. He talked about stellar decay, about the intangibility of gravity, about virtual time and black holes.

To be honest, I couldn't believe my ears and it didn't help at all when he brought out a pen and made drawings on the back of beermats, of apparatus with which they did experiments to prove that nothing can be proved any longer with perfect certainty.

He was very clear, that wasn't the point, and he would begin again each time he saw that I didn't understand it, but what he was telling me was quite simply right over my head. I understood the words, for the words were as clear as could be and moreover had something familiar about them because they would also be used occasionally in studies of fiction – ellipses, parabolas and such like – but without understanding it I was hearing the most un-imaginable things I had ever heard in years. I was confused, excited and I wished I had studied physics myself.

He chortled at the eagerness with which I listened and

made him say the same thing, over and over again.

'When I see you like this, I'm able to imagine again what those poor scientists at the beginning of the century had to go through,' he said. 'In one fell swoop the world is turned on its head and, every day again, new proof is brought along, proof of the untenability of laws with which they, as scientists, grew up. They have to look on haplessly while the age-old ideal of giving a complete and objective description of nature is dropped entirely. Because of quantum mechanics, that perfect, unblemished world has to be divided up again and in that division a field emerges suddenly, one in which the physicist himself is called into question and he is no longer able to keep his subjectivity outside the front door to the laboratory. This is still best to be seen with someone like Einstein, in the tenacity with which he attempts to keep a shattered world-picture in one piece and goes flat-out to keep a thing such as coincidence outside the realm of physics. D'you know what he said?'

'No.'

'"God doesn't throw dice!"' he said.

'Did Einstein say that?'

'Seems so.'

'Did Einstein actually believe in God?'

'Einstein in any case did not believe in coincidence, Lune.'

There was quite an uproar in my head. I tried to remember what Hugo had told me, about decay, about mirror images, free particles, the paradox of twins, the beginning and end of the universe, the limits, the uncertainty-principle and the law of increasing chaos, but I couldn't. It was all too unimaginable. That all those splendid concepts belonged in physics, this was actually the most unimaginable of all. As I listened to these and heard how Hugo used them to clarify something to me about neutrons, protons and photons, I already drew them toward me, robbing them of their meaning for the knowledge of the world of physics, in order to forge them in my head into words with which you could say something about life in general and that of the writer in particular.

'They are in fact all mathematical constructs, dreamed up,' Hugo said, 'and when we have dreamed something up we must, in order to understand something of that reality at least, act for a moment as if those constructs are real; as if it's substantial, matter, something extant in space and time. You quite simply have a faulty image of us, Lune. There are highly original chaps in this profession, you bet. They dream up silly names for those particles, a little bit mystic, too, though I don't like that kind of stuff at all.'

'Which?'

'I can't translate them. We use the English terms, *charm*, for instance, and *strangeness*. How would you translate that?'

'*Strangeness*? As a name for something thought up? A *curio*, I should say. But *charm*, *a charm*? Isn't that an amulet or something?'

'*Un charmeur* is a magician.'

'Are you a charmer?'

'Hardly,' says Hugo and for the first time I see that he, too, can feel put on the spot. Something trembles in his lower lip. He looks at me very calmly and smiles. And then he says, under his breath but I hear it, that he's more the one now who feels himself to be the victim of enchantment.

That's the moment I know that we shall become lovers. And he begins to suspect this.

It is already late when we decide to go back on to the beach one more time to look at the setting sun. The brandy has heated my blood and the cold no longer troubles me. We

135

have to go a good way through the dunes and then down a hill. I am elated and also rather scared. Of what is to come, of the nakedness and love.

Maybe that's why I don't walk but run down the hill and further, on to the beach, as well, in the direction of the red glow on the water. I feel younger than I am and very bold. I also rather feel like shouting and rolling full-length through the sand but I don't do any of these. Only when I am out of breath and halt, do I hear his footsteps behind me. I turn round. He runs like an athlete, I can see. I bend my knees, slap my thighs with my hands a few times and then spread my arms wide. Come to mummy then.

He doesn't fall for that one. He stops running, walks up to me and sweeps his arms around my legs, presses them into the backs of my knees and lifts me high up into the sky. I am forced to grasp his head.

'You're a light wee thing,' he says.

Pressed close to his body, I slip down till our faces are level. I swing my legs around his hips. I feel he wants me, too. I'm going to kiss him. I purse my lips and come closer. He doesn't make a single move with his mouth and, knowing this one by now, I press my laughing lips against his, inhale him. His lips are unexpectedly soft. I become very calm and put my cheek against his.

'Lune?'

'Yes.'

'I think I'm becoming a touch moon-sick,' he says.

'Wow!' say I.

We did hang around a bit longer, watching the sun, until he said something terrible and I wanted to go home at once. He said that the sun was decaying as well.

'The sun is slowly going out,' he said, and that then we would cease to exist. I asked him why, right this moment when I longed for eternity more than ever, he had to tell something so sad. I said that, instantly, I didn't feel like taking even one more step, setting out on something, making plans. And how he could carry on living with this knowledge.

'But it'll take another five billion years, at least,' he said, surprised.

'I really couldn't give a toss. It's nothing the less for that. An eternity is an eternity, and no end should come to it. Never.'

He was startled, I was sad. He turned my face towards him.

'It's not that you're crying about,' he said, 'it's something else.'

Sure.

On the way back we keep silent. In Amsterdam, I show him the way to my house. It's obvious. We don't need to mention it. Only when we cross the threshold of my room and I see him standing there, such a big man in my little room which is stuffed full of books, where there's paper everywhere, piles of paper, where no man really can come in without violating a relationship, the relationship with that room and those books, with the relics of my seclusion, only then do I suddenly feel like talking an awful lot, to begin talking and not stop for the time being.

He sees my desolation. He lifts me up and carries me to the bed in a corner of the room. He lays me down and sits upright beside me. He caresses my face, my forehead. Something preposterous wells up in me, I don't know why, but I have to say it.

'Hugo?' I ask, my eyes closed.

'Yes.'

'I'm going to say something odd. May I? I want to ask you something. I want to ask you to initiate me in love, for you to be my instructor. It's a perfect lie, but I now want to say to you that I'm still a virgin and haven't a clue about love. It isn't even true. I've done everything God has forbidden under the sun, for sure, but today I feel as if I'm still a virgin and have never been to bed with a man before. Can you teach me to make love?'

I open my eyes. His gaze is soft. He looks serious.

'All right,' he says.

'You don't have to talk about love,' say I, 'but you must tell me everything about your body, reveal to me what its secret is. I want to get to know it.'

Next morning, I have been watching his face a good while before he wakes up. I can't keep my eyes off him, even though I want to because I remind myself too much of a second-rate actress in a B-movie, but that's how it is, I have to look.

He wakes up the way he walks and looks, and the way he tutored me last night: calmly, fluently, as if there is no gaping chasm between dream and reality.

'Lune,' he says, languidly, and he puts his arm around me.

'Master,' say I.

'How're you feeling?' he asks.

'Mature,' I say.

We have breakfast. We are sitting at the table among the walls with books. On one of the bookshelves sits, pride of place, a picture of Mr Foucault. I'd cut out the photograph from a magazine. He is sitting behind a table on which there is a simple typewriter. In the background you can see the walls of his house, full of books. He is sitting on a wooden chair and leaning with his forearms on the edge of the table. He is completely bald and wears glasses with metal frames and rectangular lenses. He looks directly at the viewer. I look at him every day. Today I think that

138

Hugo and he resemble each other a bit, without quite seeing just now what the actual similarity is based upon.

'Are you still busy with Foucault?' asks Hugo when he sees the photo.

'I desire him as well,' I say, laughing. 'You brought in your own rival here.'

'I was afraid of that,' he says.

Hugo asks me why I am studying philosophy. I dawdle answering. I hesitate whether I will say: 'In order to practise dying,' or: 'Because I long for a personal destiny.' Both replies are equally beautiful. Both are not my own, either. They're really too good to be true.

'In order to learn to live,' I say in the end, without knowing that someone else has also put it that way once upon a time. I only find that out later on.

'Aren't you able to, then?'

'What?'

'Live.'

'No,' I say, 'I'm not good enough at it.'

He asks me if I'm then able to learn this from someone like Foucault.

'From Foucault, yes, and from you.'

From whom else?

Until the morning of the funeral we leave the house only once, to buy food. After that, we stay inside. The stove's turned up high. It's nice and sultry inside the house.

He can lie, sleep, stare, read in bed for hours on end, motionless. I am more restless, get up regularly, go and sit at my table so that I can look at him, and I try to study a little.

Sometimes he calls me to him.

'Lune, come and lie here with me a while; I've got something else to teach you.'

I did ask him whether he had been adulterous before. He said he hadn't. I asked what Sybille would have to say about this.

'She'll break every bone in my body,' he said.

'Are you going to tell her?' I ask.

'Yes,' he says.

I do feel shame, but it never lasts for long. I tell him it's all due to him, to his imperturbability and also to the darkness of his face which is so hermetic you can only discern anything from it with difficulty.

'All I understand about you,' I say to him, 'is in your body. Not even in its shape but in its tempo, in the duration of your movements, in the silence between the succeeding gestures.' I tell him that that's what attracts me most in him, his tempo.

'You're so earthly,' I say, 'so linear. What in heaven's name is it you seek up there among those stars?'

He says he envies me.

'You have a word for everything,' he says. 'Miel always used to say that you have the constellation of a writer, but that you yourself don't want to put your shoulders into it.'

It hurts to hear that. Hugo sees this. He begins to caress me, slowly, devotedly. I feel like crying. I relish the heavy feeling and the trouble it costs me to speak now, but I speak. I tell him of the resistance, of the seeking and waiting, that I don't want to yet, cannot yet, that it is as if I first must know everything, must get to know everything and, in particular, must unlearn a lot of things, try out a lot of things, the possibilities. That you can be so many things, so much is possible. That I should never want to write from a shortage of possibilities, but precisely the opposite, because I had chosen from a wealth of them. I don't know. I can't quite grasp it either. It's really all too mad for words.

140

I try to keep talking for as long as possible, in the face of the superior strength of the body. Hugo leans on his elbow. He caresses me and looks at me. He listens. I also look at him as I talk, cry. It's a battle. I must keep my breath up, near my head, my voice.

'That's why I have to learn,' I say. 'I must not make mistakes, that's what it's all about really, this too, this thing with you, too. I can't explain properly. It's very close-by, the answer is, yet it eludes me time and again. It'll come, won't it?'

Then my tummy demands all of my breath.

'Shall we just run through all possible disasters and do the sad bit together?' I ask him during the last night.

'It can only be an incident, Lune. There's nothing else for it.'

I keep a stiff upper lip. You can't keep on bawling all the time, that gets boring. But I won't bear incidents, when it comes down to it. What is an incident? A one-off, something piffling, an occurrence with no meaning, without value.

'Is that it?' I ask with anger, 'an insignificant occurrence?'

'You know yourself that now you're talking piffle,' Hugo answers just as calmly as ever, 'that that is not what I want to say.'

'D'you know what *is* piffle, Hugo? An incident, now that's real piffle.'

'Unfortunate choice of words,' he says. 'You shouldn't trip me up on words. Rather tell me what you want. Come on, tell me. What does Lune dream of?'

We're laughing again. I feel myself to be a tamed shrew.

'D'you know what I dream of? Of the repeating, the repeating of an endless series of incidents.'

141

The next morning is the first time Hugo wakes up earlier than me. He calls me. I hear him in the distance. He says I must wake up, that we have to go East, the funeral.

It's a voice on yonder side, but I don't know what I must do to get there too, on the other side, with him. I have forgotten how to part my eyelids, how to pass on the signal with my brains. That's where the impotence is, in the connection between my mind and my face.

I feel how he lifts me, draws my limp body on to his lap and rocks me.

'You seemed dead, almost,' he says later on.

I'm not doing too well at calculus today. I cannot manage to end up with thirty-three and I give up counting when we enter the cemetery. Time has condensed to an eternity in a day, it has run away with me and must now go back into the regimentation of dates.

It is January 30th, 1984. Hugo returns by the 16.45 train to Paris, arrives Gare du Nord at 21.45 and is awaited there by Sybille. Just prior to our departure for Hengelo he has phoned her. She was fuming and worried. She had rung the hotel several times, in vain.

'*Je te dirai*,' Hugo says, 'later on.'

Later on – in retrospect everything becomes comprehensible.

It is terrible to have to bury someone.

Mrs Van Eysden is already standing at the edge of the hole in the earth. The coffin rests on a wooden framework above the hole. She does not look at the coffin but at the hole, underneath. The wait is for everyone to have gathered around the grave. The funeral director gives a sign to the priest when the moment has come and the priest reads the prayers from a book. Then the funeral director

142

nods to Mrs Van Eysden as a sign that it's over.

She shakes her head. She points at the coffin. The funeral director looks questioningly at her for he does not understand what she wishes to convey.

I do. Hugo does too. Hugo puts an arm around me.

We see Mrs Van Eysden walk across to the surprised man and we hear how she says, calmly and in a clear voice:

'You must lower the coffin into the earth, now, in my presence.'

It is outdated to lower the coffin into the earth in the presence of everyone. The funeral director, in whispered tones, wants to make something clear to her, about the altered ritual.

'He is my only son and I want you to bury the coffin in the earth now,' she says.

She turns round. She considers the matter closed and returns to her place at the edge of the grave. It is as if she is thinking very deeply about something. There is an expression of concentration on her face.

The men who carried the bier to the cemetery approach and request the people around the coffin to move aside a little. We are among these as well, Hugo and I. I know he thinks so, too, that we must all face it out together and must keep on looking to the end.

The pallbearers take up the ends of the tapes which have been strung underneath the coffin. They take the tape on to their shoulders. The funeral director takes away the flowers and the funeral cloth from the coffin and calls in another man's assistance to take away the wooden frame. But Mrs Van Eysden has already bent forwards and she heaves at one of the planks.

It starts to rain again.

The only sound we hear is the groaning of the mother of the astrologer. She groans with effort.

By pulling on the tapes the bearers keep the coffin up.

When they ease the tapes, the coffin disappears slowly into the earth. Mrs Van Eysden looks up. She is looking for something. Apart from the group, two men stand with spades in their hands. She discovers them and walks over to them. She asks one of the men if she might have the spade. Those men don't know what's hit them either and hand her their spades almost simultaneously. Spade in hand, she returns to the grave and begins to dig furiously in the fresh earth.

Chapter VI

THE ARTIST

No matter how hard I think about it, I can no longer work out what brought me on to the trail of Lucas Asbeek and saw to it that his name lodged itself in my head and stayed there, for years.

Was it Anton Pasman's novel, *The Artist*, dedicated to him? Was it one of his sculptures which had made him so famous in the sixties? Was it an interview in one of the Dutch newspapers which I tore out, put away safely and lost, but which I recalled at times and for which I searched all the files because I was certain it had to be hidden somewhere?

The keystone, in any case, was the documentary *The betrayal of things*, broadcast on Saturday, March 23rd, 1985, six days before I would take my Master's finals.

Suddenly everything came together.

Whether this is the beginning, I don't know. It must have been October, an autumnal day with much wind and rain. It was then 1982, that much is certain, for I had decided to stop working in the antiquariat on Friday afternoons.

Sometimes in life things do occur which have a clear beginning and end, with an opening and a close, rounded incidents, having the structure of a tale.

I was reminded of this when I was sitting there and waiting for closing time to come. Because the friendship between the astrologer and myself had begun in the shop, I had asked him to come and collect me around six. Together, we would celebrate the end of the Pijp-days and have something to eat somewhere in town.

This had made him happy.

I am sitting there for the last time and then that man comes in.

He's wearing a faded-green raincoat and has a worn leather briefcase in his hand. His thick, grey hair is wet with rain. He has pale-blue eyes.

Something happens to me when I see him, something fierce and unheard-of, it paralyses me with fear and desire, all at once. It is abnormal.

He has the face in its most perfect form.

I have sought him.

The antiquariat is small: a living room full of books, more or less. There is barely any space to walk. How oppressively narrow it is here, how closely packed upon one another you are, only dawns on me once he is inside.

The stove is burning.

He greets me with a brief nod of his head and a glance which lasts too long for the purpose. There's something mixed about it, it's a flash of a battle between reserve and openness.

I remain seated and hardly dare move.

He looks around the place, takes a book from the shelf with translated novels, leafs through it a little and takes a seat on the stool beside the stove. That stool's always there. I've never known anyone to sit down on it. He isn't bothered by a thing. He reads. He sits there, very relaxed.

I don't know how to get some air and I choke with

tension. The space is too small for the two of us and I fear that something is going to happen, something inevitable.

But nothing does.

After a while, he gets up and steps up to my table. He puts the book he was reading down in front of me. He wishes to buy it. I look in the back to see how much it is. It's as if I'm blind, my eyes won't make headway and stay glued to the first figure. I can no longer read. According to me, it all takes a long time and I'm behaving strangely.

I drone the figure out loud and he gives me money. I must give change but I don't remember having made a calculation. According to me I've just put down any sum of money on the table, pot luck.

When he draws the door shut behind him, I am sitting on my chair, defeated, relieved and deserted. It's still too soon, it occurs to me, to be meeting him. I'm not ready for it yet.

Suddenly, I am dead tired.

That evening, I told the astologer about it, but he could tell me no more than that my Moon rendered me very receptive that day. Fat lot of good that was to me.

I wanted to know who that man was.

I said to the astrologer that I would meet him again, to be sure.

'What has to be, has to be,' said he.

The teapot and the window were part of the permanent collection of a museum in the centre of the country. I didn't know much about sculpture and if you don't know much about it, you see less in art.

With the work of Lucas Asbeek things were different.

I saw it and understood it in a way I had only understood poetry till then, intuitively, totally and nearly always without being able to explain to someone else what exactly was so affecting about it.

Likewise, too, with the teapot. It was, I think, because of the words and the handwriting. Lucas described things.

The teapot stood on a plinth over which a tea-towel with blue and white checks had been draped. At a distance it seemed an ordinary teapot, one of those pot-bellied ones, very touching and, all on its own, it was capable of evoking an entire family tableau.

Only when you came closer could you see how Asbeek had managed to magically transform the innocent teapot into a kind of instrument of torture. The end of the spout had changed from a yawning, generous little mouth into two embittered lips, clenched shut, and the lid had been bonded to the pot with big, fat dollops of glue. The sole opening through which some of the contents might get out was a tiny, inverted spout situated exactly above the handle. What at first sight seemed a sweet design of little pink stripes turned out at close quarters to be the endlessly repeated sentence; 'Don't be afraid, darling, if it's in there it'll also come out.'

I thought it painfully beautiful.

The window was in one of the lobbies of the museum. It was a big, upright window frame. The two panes had been worked in such a manner that it appeared as if they were permanently misted over and someone, with his finger tip, had just written something in the condensation. By sliding the right pane behind the left, the two texts on the windows merged and together they would form the negation of what they asserted independently.

I would always forget what was written there, exactly.

When I visited the museum from time to time, I repeatedly resolved to copy down the texts, but once I was there I'd again be enchanted by Asbeek's handwriting and then I'd decide there was no point in only taking the texts back home with me.

Not only Lucas Asbeek's things were the ones to remind me of reading poetry. Lucas Asbeek himself, too, had a different effect on me than other artists. No statue, painting, photograph, film or composition had ever aroused a longing for its maker in me, while every good book evoked, besides admiration, that impossible, irrational desire for the writer as well. Behind the teapot and the window a poet was hiding, according to me, and it was the poet who, one day, somewhere, I would meet again.

The interview is not to be found. I no longer know which newspaper it was in, who the journalist was and when it appeared. It made an impression on me and I can no longer even say why. I vaguely recall the gist of the interview and even then primarily because of the strange photograph of Asbeek printed alongside it.

There was nothing more to be seen of him than the back of his head, his neck, his shoulders and part of his back. He wore a gentleman's hat and he was looking up at the sky. By the look of things he was a very big man.

In the interview, he says not to want to be photographed because the artist as an individual has nothing to do with the work. A good work of art is one that touches on truth and you can never credit the person with truth: truth bears no name tag. According to Lucas Asbeek, all art ought to be as anonymous as the truth.

I did look for indications as to his love-life, for the names of women, children, girlfriends, but I didn't find them. The piece was about roaming, seeking, art, and heavy things.

Anton Pasman's novel is about those too. Called *The Artist*, it is about the friendship between a painter (Simon) and a writer (Philip). The painter thinks too much about painting and that's why he's no longer able to paint, and the writer thinks an awful lot about writing, too, but at least he does write a book about it.

The Artist is dedicated to Lucas Asbeek, and of course I know that you must never allow a character to coincide completely with an existing person, the way you must not identify the narrator as being the author, either, but I read the novel as were it about Lucas Asbeek's life and Anton Pasman had barely invented anything.

What must have been invented, definitely, was Simon's death. Pasman has him commit suicide on the morning of his fifty-seventh birthday. Philip, the writer, finds him in his garret in the Pijp, dangling lifeless between heaven and earth. A ticket hangs from his toe. Simon has written on it: 'So I discovered truth after all. I am who I am. Not to be lived with, frankly.'

It was Simon's death in *The Artist* which gave me the idea for my Master's thesis.

It was too late to become an adherent of a different philosophy, just before the finishing line like, but to be honest the word 'Text' had begun to bore me by and by in no mean way. It was too little, there was more, but it was a prescribed kind of thought I had not been able to get away from. I dreaded ranging myself among the growing ranks of students who produced one paper after another about the claustrum of the text, the death of the author and the scripturalness of life.

The idea had no longer been original for ages and I would have liked to have thought something different in due course, but this I had not done. Together with the others I had begun to regard Sartre as being unreadable and had been fascinated by Mr Derrida. The question as to why we were all obsessed by the same ideas occupied me most of all, but I didn't have enough time to answer it. All of a sudden I was in a hurry. I wanted to be shot of school. It was getting time to go out into the open.

If I wasn't ready for it now I probably never would be.

I had to tell Guido de Waeterlinck my plans for my Master's thesis and that was how I came to be talking for the first time about the obsession which had been growing rampant all those years, the passion for an unknown man whom I only knew through some images, the newspapers and a novel. That's what it would have to be about, one way or another, I said to Guido.

He then spoke of the reclusive power of adoration, about intercession, triangular relationships and how adoration is a sincere need of the religious human being. And he said something about idols and stars. They were said to have assumed the function of priests and saints; nowadays we were only able to maintain contact with the sacred by means of idols, because we ascribed to them a link with the divine.

'So you see,' Guido said, 'your desire for this Lucas Asbeek is again a disguised form of your longing to engage with the sacred.'

The sweetie.

The only other one with whom I ever spoke about Lucas Asbeek was Daniel Daalmeyer. This came about because Daniel told me something about his father's art collection. He couldn't see anything in most works of art, but he would liked to have Lucas Asbeek's *The Angel* hanging above his bed. This was a chubby, baroque, gold-coloured cherub. Instead of the usual downward and compassionate gaze on to the terrestrial mêlée, this cherub looked pleadingly upward. The banner held aloft read: 'How about revealing yourself for once . . .'

I was startled upon hearing his name and hesitated as to

whether I should reveal myself and this preposterous obsession, but it was uncontrollable and before I knew it I had already asked Daniel Daalmeyer whether he knew Lucas Asbeek personally.

Daniel would rarely give an answer without first having asked a counter-question, and in order to obtain an answer I had to tell him about the teapot and the window, about the newspaper and the novel. I tried to keep a grip on myself and not to sound like a idolising fanatic, but Daniel has a keen eye and very soon he had the scornful look in his eyes with which he so often regarded me.

Like so many artists, Lucas Asbeek had been one of his father's patients and, again like so many grateful artist-patients, had given him one of his works of art. He didn't know Lucas Asbeek personally and, alas, he was not in a position to act as an intermediary on my behalf.

'It's time I became famous, too,' Daniel had added. 'Fame eroticises and there's nothing that fans the flames of women's rescue-fantasies more than a gloomy artist.'

I desperately wanted to believe in Guido de Waeterlinck's interpretation, but I relied more on Daniel's. It was more unpleasant and thus more true.

This is an odd trait.

I noticed it for the first time with reflections in a mirror. The mirror in which I rediscover myself as podgy, bloated, wilted, drab, flabby and ugly, betrays in one fell swoop the flattering deceit of all the preceding reflections, and my opinion of the most repulsive reflection will be that it is the one which reveals the representation of myself that has the greatest veracity.

Art and life, semblance and reality, lies and truth, *The Artist* is about these age-old couplings. Through the dialogues between the author and the painter and the sentences with which Simon took leave of life, I ended up with another pairing, Plato and Socrates, the writer and the character.

For the first time in ages, I reread *Socrates' Apologia* and then I suddenly believed myself able to understand what life's all about.

Writing begins with the cessation of every other movement, with sitting still, staying inside. I sat down and wrote, for days on end, for weeks. I wrote about Socrates and Plato, about Mary and the Trinity, about Anton Pasman and Lucas Asbeek, about the writer's fate and that of the character, about the curious meaning of proper names, about the fear of publishing something, of exhibiting it or crossing the frontier between the personal and the public in another way, by means of an object.

I ransacked everything, and during the writing I barely opened a book.

I didn't even know any more where I got it all from.

One night it was finished and I hadn't a clue whether it was good or bad, literature or philosophy, true or made-up.

On an impulse, that very same night, I dialled the number of Guido de Waeterlinck. He answered in a sleepy voice.

'It's finished,' I said and then I cried for several minutes. I had difficulty stopping.

'Now I know what writing is,' I said to Guido.

'And is it what you wanted?'

'If it has to be so, then this'll be the only thing I'll ever want.'

That he understood.

'Better get some sleep now, poppet.'

Next day he read my piece. I sat in on this and looked on as he read. After a few pages I noticed he had forgotten my presence, more or less. Suddenly I was happy.

We sat there like that, together. It was a sacred hour, for at that moment we were taking leave of one another and we knew it. He knew it while reading and I knew it as I saw him read what I had written.

From time to time he would smile and then I would know why.

An hour later he turns the final page. He looks up, looks at me and says: 'Marie Deniet.'

'Here,' say I.

'Welcome to the world of books,' Guido says, a little sadly, and now I too am a little sad, but that's how it should be and it is pleasant.

'But now at last it's perhaps time for you to cease your dogged attempts to escape from what you are,' Guido says softly. 'What you have written here is after all an apologia for being a writer. What then are you still looking for in order to justify the choice of being a writer?'

'That which I don't yet know,' I reply, 'love.'

It is not the garnering of knowledge which is the greatest spur behind the decision at eighteen to continue learning instead of going to work, but obtaining deferment and the concomitant freedom to doubt. The things you defer are the choices with which people wish to meet their desires to bind themselves and to be unfree.

For the first time, I myself was no longer someone who lived in the freedom of deferment, a freedom that until now had made me someone who was no one yet, but all the time busy becoming someone. The postponement had ended. I was no longer anybody. The only thing I still had to look forward to was the ritual conclusion to the postponement itself.

The date for defending my thesis had been set for March

29th. There were three weeks between the time upon which Guido read my thesis and the day of the examination itself. Emptiness needed no longer than that to take possession of me. Time made me hollow and paralysed me. I was one absent, unreal and without any meaning.

First having roamed the city a bit, aimlessly, I locked the door to my room one day, drew the curtains, unplugged the phone and the door bell and left the mail lying in the hallway. I crept into bed and might as well have been dead.

It happened and I had no defence.

I knew what it was: it was the fall. The falling had started on the sly and I didn't know how to call a halt to it.

A number of days prior to the examination taking place, I got up. It was a Saturday morning. I had eaten and drunk little, and I was feeling dizzy. I washed and dressed, reconnected the phone and the door bell, and looked in the kitchen for a shopping bag.

The sound of the telephone ringing startled me. Before picking up the receiver, I cleared my throat a few times and practised out loud saying 'hello'. It was my worried mother. She asked where I had been; she'd rung so frequently.

'Just away from it all,' I said, 'a quiet week: I needed that.'

I tried to sound cheerful but speaking caused me difficulty. She told me about all who would be coming to Amsterdam to add splendour to my party. She asked whether I had also thought about Easter, the week after the party.

I hadn't.

'But of course I'll be coming,' I said.

After having put down the receiver, I actually felt something for once: gratitude, a having been rescued. My mother had lent a name to time and had made me the

155

person I had always been, at least, and always would be: a daughter, a sister. I needn't do anything for that. I was this unquestionably.

I hesitated whether I would ring her back in order to say something uncommonly nice to her, something really sentimental. I didn't. She'd only worry. We're not that sentimentally inclined, back home.

I was hungry.

The neighbour from one floor down had left the mail on the bottom step of the stairs in a neat little pile. I left it untouched. This was my most immediate future, something to be able to return home for in a moment.

Outside, the sunlight hurt my eyes. The mild breeze made them water. I couldn't care less. I hadn't made up my eyes anyway.

I bought fresh bread, butter, cheese and, exceptionally so, a newspaper. After this I concluded that I had been out for long enough and turned on my heels to head back. This first little excursion had made me dead-tired and I began to realise how great is the power of emptiness.

It was on the television page among the programme previews. *The betrayal of things* was being described as an intriguing documentary about two artists who had once garnered much fame in a short time and of whom little had subsequently been heard again. One of the artists was the poet Nel Vat, the other the sculptor Lucas Asbeek.

I didn't know how to get through the rest of the day.

The first image was that of a very beautiful elderly woman. She was sitting, ramrod straight, at an antique desk in a room full of knick-knacks. The walls were hung with oil-paintings of still-lives. Above her head hung a portrait of herself. She was writing. She wore spectacles attached to which there was a silver-coloured chain. You could hear a mantel-clock ticking.

The next image was one of Lucas Asbeek's back. I had seen it before. He was sitting in the grass on the bank of a river. He was staring across the water and didn't move. The camera zoomed in and panned ninety degrees so Asbeek's profile came into shot.

His was the face in its most perfect form, the face that belonged to the man I had seen in the antiquariat in the Pijp, years before, the man with the pale-blue eyes who, in an inexplicable way, had upset me so much.

It suddenly seemed natural to me, this unlikely coincidence of events.

Nel Vat talked a mile a minute, fascinatingly, wittily and in careful formulations. She had become fearful of people, she told.

'Lucas Asbeek didn't really like the fame, I think, but I thought all that attention was wonderful. I relished it intensely. People were absolutely delighted with my poems and I was most grateful for this, that they were so fond of them. Nowadays, people no longer like the poems and they no longer like me, either. Sometimes the phone doesn't ring for an entire week. I find it incomprehensible, but I *have* to write, there's nothing else for it.

'Yet it did look so promising for me. Do *you* understand why life should then take such a dramatic turn?'

As lively as she was, so inwardly quiet were the images of Lucas Asbeek. He barely said a word and that which he did say was vague and pervaded with doubt.

You saw how he went for a walk, ate, read, or just stared at the sky a bit. He was surrounded by an impenetrable loneliness. You forgot he was being followed by a camera and was being seen, something which provoked a contradiction between sincerity and pose: Lucas Asbeek was

157

showing how unseen was the way he lived.

After the broadcast I was devastated, and I was ashamed.

On the morning of March 29th, I woke up alone. At first, I wasn't aware of it at all, but after an hour or two I was so nervous I couldn't even remember the title of my thesis. Plato, Derrida? Never heard of them.

The examination would take place at two in the afternoon, in public, the way I had emphatically desired it to be. Now I wondered why I inflicted such things on myself and I sought ways to undo this decision even now, to ring everybody, to cancel and, like every other student, to defend my piece behind closed doors, in the safe presence of Guido de Waeterlinck and his seconds.

To be honest, I didn't really even want that anymore. I was no philosopher anyhow. The only thing I had ended up with during the writing was writing itself, with something as curious as style. The style had demanded the greatest courage, but hobbling along on the pegleg of style alone, I could be nothing more than a knobbled philosopher, an exegete, a slavish hermeneutist, journalist of the theory of ideas. And this I didn't want to be.

I knew this all along, you know.

By one o'clock they were all there: my parents and brothers, Daniel, Clemens, Aaron, Ilda, Kat. I was the sole absentee. I had to remind myself continually of my own existence.

We walked to the Oudemanhuispoort. Hoping for some pathos, I tried to think very hard about now going into the university building for the last time, about leaving a world, being about to conclude a phase, but this didn't touch me.

On the square another group of people gathered around a student. They went up the stairs to the first floor more or

158

less simultaneously to us and while this boy's guests arranged themselves in front of the door to the examination hall on the right side of the corridor, mine poured inside and took their seats on the chairs set out in readiness for them.

Guido entered the hall the way I had seen him enter the lecture theatre a hundred times before. He stepped up to me and greeted me with a kiss. He shook hands with my parents and my brothers. He, too, was nervous.

This made me calmer.

Someone would have to keep a cool head here.

'Well, we'd better begin,' Guido said, and he closed the door.

An hour later I was standing outside, my praises sung, wreathed in laurels, cool as a cucumber, unaffected and wet through. Aaron had opened a bottle of champagne and most of its contents had ended up on my chest.

I was tired and soulless. The sounds around me seemed to be coming from far away and were only getting through to me with difficulty.

In the hallway there was a table with booze around which the other graduate's guests were thronging already. The champagne glass was empty and I walked up to the table to pour myself a glass of wine.

I looked up and saw him.

He was standing a little aside from the group of people, and was regarding them.

His grey hair was cut very short.

I stared at him, frozen, and continued to stand like this, I don't know how long for. His glass was empty; he turned his head toward the table. He saw me. He looked around to see whether there was someone else who was holding my gaze like that. There wasn't. Surprised, he turned his face back toward me. I looked him in the face, there was

159

nothing else I could do. He walked up to me.

'Ought I to know you?' he asked.

'No,' I said, 'I know *you*.'

Then I said: 'I've been looking for you a long time already.'

I could say everything, without shame, I could take anything too. I was in no-man's-land, an intermediate area where no laws are in effect and everyone is inviolable. I did not wish to keep or bring along anything of the past, and no start had yet been made on a future I would have to protect scrupulously. I had nothing to lose.

'How come?'

'I share a kind of history with you, but I can't tell you all that now.'

'Are you a student here?'

'No, not any more.'

I told him how I had taken my finals just now. He told me that a young friend of his had just done so, too, taking something terribly difficult, he said, something to do with Kant. He asked me what mine had been.

'You,' I said, 'people like you.'

He scratched his head with his fingers.

'What's all this?'

'The seduction scene,' I replied, 'Act One: the mystery.'

He laughed, as did I. Because of the laughter, something stirred itself free in my tummy, from underneath the stones, a pleasure and an excitement which made me suddenly become even more nervous than during the hours prior to the exam. It got through to me that I was leaving school, was finished and ready, for him too, for that other life, the real life – with him.

By his eyes I saw that he was confused, suspicious and curious, all at once. His eyelids were slightly swollen and red-rimmed.

'You're sorrowful,' I said.

160

'I'm desperate,' he said to that, immediately. He didn't know whether he ought to have said this. He looked panicky.

'Yes, you're in despair.'

'Might we make a date? Then you can tell me all about people like me.'

'Fine.'

'So when?'

'Saturday.'

'Tomorrow?'

'Yes, tomorrow.'

'No,' he said, 'in that case I'd rather the following Saturday.'

'Where?'

'*Arti*?'

'All right, I'll be there at nine.'

Glass in hand, I walked back to my guests. I was weak-kneed and my hands were shaking.

'The nerves are only showing properly now, according to me,' my mother said when I went and stood next to her, 'you're all pale and shaky. Did you know that man?'

'Yes,' I said, and went silent.

'So who was he then?' asked my boundlessly intrepid mother.

'A character,' said I.

'No, tell me, seriously now,' she said.

'Your prospective son-in-law,' I said, seriously.

'That man? Child, he could be your father!'

'Could have been,' I said, and moreover I added that I wouldn't be able to come home for Easter.

I love him, I thought, I'll rescue him. Perhaps that's my destiny. You've got to do something, haven't you? A fruitless existence, now who'd ever want that?

161

In Lucas I would be undertaking my first and most important Socratic field-work, lay bare the contradictions in his thinking, reconcile him once again with art by explaining to him why he, if he actually did coincide with Simon from *The Artist*, could indeed not be an artist and that his ideas formed an obstacle to his actions. The way Clemens Brandt had wanted to break into the story of the fall of man, thus it frequently had happened to me in reading *The Artist* that I had wanted to join the writer and the painter in order to say to Simon what the writer was neglecting to. This being impossible, I had written it all down in my thesis.

I mustn't forget to bring along the thesis this evening. If I lost my way I would always still be able to read a passage from my own work.

At times I cannot remember too well all that I have thought up.

Arti is a private club. To be able to go in you have to be a member. Lucas Asbeek had promised to wait for me outside, then to accompany me in as his guest.

He was standing in the lobby and looking at the posters pinned up on the walls. The previous Saturday he had been wearing a two-piece suit with a shirt and tie. A faint smell of mothballs had hung around him. Now he was wearing boys' clothes: jeans and a short jacket in a bright green colour.

'Hello.'

'Hey, hello,' he said with almost childish joy. He took my hand and shook it unthinkingly roughly which made me laugh. He looked me in the face for only a very short while, a brief, searching and slightly timid glance, turned round and, talking the while, preceded me to the doors which gave entrance to the club.

'It *is* good you've come,' he said. 'I do think it rather an

162

odd appointment. This week I began to doubt myself more and more, whether we actually had arranged anything for today, I mean. Happily you're here and it's all really true.'

He walked with a stoop, a little woodenly and with his right shoulder drawn up. He walked in the manner of someone who has no notion at all of his appearance, his gait. Never corrected, never been made to hear something about himself. As he spoke he gestured with his hands, faint garlands in the air which made those big hands suddenly become very feminine.

There was a guests' register on a table by the entrance. Lucas Asbeek wrote his name down and then handed me the pen. I had to write my name and address. Bent over the book, I looked at the handwriting and the signature I knew so well. It excited me to be so close to the name only so recently written down. I felt strange, unreal, at bursting point. In writing my name beneath his, it was as if the real and the unreal were being riveted together, as if I, together with him, was signing the register in law, was making a marriage bond with someone from my imagination, from my dream, from the lonely engagement with letters and images. The unbelievable realness almost hurt and I would have liked best to have frozen in this bent-over position to allow the sensation to continue for as long as possible.

Lucas walked over to a table to one side in the room. In the middle there were round, wooden tables, on the walls paintings were hanging in broad, ornate frames. There were mainly old people in the place. I saw Lucas, going over to the bar to fetch us something to drink, greet several of them.

I didn't know what to do with myself and took my thesis from my bag. With a fountain pen I wrote 'For Lucas Asbeek' on the inside of the cover and put it down on his side of the table.

With trembling hands, Lucas set down the glasses of wine on the table. The skin of his hands had some small, red, slightly flaky spots.

'Is this for me?' he asked when he saw the thesis lying there. 'How kind. Thanks.'

'*The fate of a character*, Marie Deniet,' he read out loud. 'Once again, I've been rescued,' he added, laughing, 'for, to be honest, I didn't know your name any more. Did I actually ever know it? Whatever – I then ended up writing "young woman N.N." in my diary, but Marie is better. Cheers.'

He leafed through my thesis; a moment later he was reading. His eyes were glued to the page and when he did look at me again he had a devastated look in his eyes. I could imagine what he had been reading.

'It sucks me in immediately,' he said. 'According to me, it's about all sorts of things I rack my brains silly about. Could you give the plot away to me and tell me what Socrates' fate is, in the end?'

'To be a character and end up in a story.'

'Like me,' he said.

'Like you,' said I.

'What are we really doing here?' he said and looked at me with weary pity. 'I don't like *Arti* at all – do you? In fact, I'd like to go home, best of all. You must understand that I have to read this now. Shall we go?'

We went. We opted for the house closest by. Mine. There, he went and sat at my desk, read and stayed.

During the night he held me in his arms and said that we matched, darling. See, we matched. It felt like the embrace of fate and fate was love and love came by the name of Lucas Asbeek. I wasn't even that surprised.

In the morning, I slipped carefully from his arms and drew up a chair to the bed. I watched. I shook the length

164

and breadth of my body. *Tremor nervosa*, thought I.

He lay there like a young god, so perfect, unblemished, a hand resting gently against his cheek, the other in a fist in front of his chest. There was a hint of a smile around his mouth. You laugh, you're satisfied. It's right like this, at last. The smile seemed to be one that properly belonged to waking so that, for a moment, I distrusted him and thought that he was feigning sleep, but when I bent forwards in order to be able to look more accurately at the details of his face, nothing changed in this attitude. He slept, deeply.

That night, I had discovered the red spots of his hands on other parts of his body, too.

'Psoriasis?' I had asked.

'Yes.'

'Hallmark of ambiguous hyper-individualists,' I had said.

'Sure,' he said.

His face was smooth, he had fewer wrinkles than I did. Old age had hidden itself somewhere behind his ear, in the neighbourhood of the soft lobes, hidden to those who had no business there.

I searched everywhere. I wanted to end up on every spot.

After he had woken up, I boiled him an egg and wished him a happy Easter.

The rest of my life had begun.

I then did not know yet that László would turn out to be right and that I am indeed one of those who become ill with love.

'Shall I tell you when our history together began?'

'No, don't bother, Marie. Our history together begins today.'

'Don't you like them, histories?'

'Oh yes, but I don't want to be a character in your tale,

165

part of an intrigue, junction to a plot. You can't turn me into a tale; it never accords with reality anyway.'

'Tales are not intended to do that, to accord with reality.'

'I'm afraid of artifice.'

'You're afraid of art, Lucas.'

'It's a strange encounter, this one with you. You please me. Only now do I realise that for the first time I'm talking with someone about sense and meaning, and this while I have always been occupied with such things. But it is indeed difficult to talk about it. With you, one has to. With you at least I have a dialogue.'

'We see things differently, you and I.'

'Yes, indeed we do.'

'You're like Socrates, you refuse to be a character in someone else's tale. You refuse to receive because you think you are able to be someone all on your own, completely separate from others.'

'Absolutely.'

'But perhaps that's also why you can no longer make works of art, Lucas, even though it would be your dearest wish, nevertheless, to do so again. You're as incapable of doing it as Socrates was of writing down his philosophy. You try to prevent people according you a meaning which you haven't asked for yourself, but surely this is unavoidable? Meaning is something you have to yield control over. You cannot continue to stand alongside it and say: this is what I, Lucas Asbeek, mean, and the things I make mean this and that, nothing else. You have to hand over, dare to be absent as an artist.'

'But I wish for nothing more!'

'If I'm to believe *The Artist*, it is precisely this which you're no longer able to do, to make things which you have to leave to people who, separate from you, will give

166

meaning to it.'

'That Simon is a horror. I'm not Simon. He's Anton's character. I, myself, am someone different.'

'So why is it you can no longer make any works of art?'

'Art doesn't touch upon the truth.'

'People are creatures of meaning. They huddled together, in time they started to talk with one another, out of necessity, they gave things and each other a name and since then meaning has existed, since the time it was possible to say Tom to one and Harry to the other. There is no truth of Tom and Harry at all, but along with the names came the desire for distinction, a desire for truth – that it might actually mean something to be Tom or Harry.

'Now we're no longer animals, not by a long chalk, and we continue to search for meaning and sense. It's a curse and at the same time it's beautiful, all futility.'

'So what about animals then?'

'Animals are hungry.'

'So am I,' he said and he snatched a biscuit. He put it in his mouth and looked at me fixedly as he chewed. He continued to look and he continued to stuff his mouth with biscuits, one after the other.

In his eyes glinted the mischief of the taunt and the pride of resistance. Poor Lucas. I talk incessantly. It is terrorism, the mad rage of love.

I say nothing. I look.

'There, now I'm no longer hungry.' The little dish was empty.

'Yes you are,' say I. 'You now have a disgustingly full stomach but your soul still hungers for purpose.'

Can't I please keep my mouth shut, just for once?

'Yesterday I was with that old friend of mine, a sculptor. He said something that struck home to me very much. He said you must do it for yourself, sculpting, it's something which has to be meaningful in itself, the making. And that the rest, everything surrounding it, is a circus, tosh. It has nothing to do with sculpting. I believe he's right about that.'

'I don't. You can eat and drink for yourself, and gather knowledge, but art, according to me, cannot purely and solely be something for yourself. Isn't art, with a bit of luck, also a choice for a way of dealing with others, with the entire world?

'You can reach the world by means of a thing, a statue, a book, and you can talk with the world without having to be there in person. You're there and at the same time you are not, only the thing is there and by means of this thing you make a connection between your own existence and that of everyone else. You have to dare to be mediated for by something other than yourself, something which nevertheless bears your name.'

'Sounds very true again.'

'Assuming it's true, Lucas, then it would mean that you can no longer make sculptures because you refuse to embark upon a relationship with the others. Didn't it please you? Were you really so shaken by the fame and the applause?'

'It's never enough.'

'What isn't?'

'The applause; it's never enough. And because it's not enough and the shortfall is even far worse than the applause itself, I'd rather not bother altogether, I think. I believe that's what it is. I don't want to suffer under the desire for even more.'

'It's just like love.'

'How's that?'

'We can never get enough of that, either.'

'Surely everyone's an artist. The myths about great artists are precisely so pernicious, for people are frightened off because of these myths, and it's put over on them that they're not capable of making anything themselves. It's depicted too much as being something special. People are being deprived by the myths of art and the personal glorification of artists, and I refuse to connive in that any longer.'

'Of course everybody is an artist, but not everyone exhibits, publishes, performs in public, that's the difference. In my view, you're an artist when you're able to let go of things you've made. For as long as you leave your doleful poems, revealing diaries, your paintings or your windmills made from matchsticks hidden in the sideboard, you have nothing to do with the others. You become an artist when you cross the frontier, step over the threshold to the public. Only then do you enable the world to give meaning to something.'

'But you don't need the world, do you?'

'Maybe the world needs you.'

'Why no, there's nobody out there waiting for Lucas Asbeek.'

'Oh, indeed there is, Lucas. I'm out there. I'm waiting for you, my love.'

'At times you speak like an oracle, Marie. Then I do feel that it's true what you're saying and that you mean well with me, but I don't understand a word of it.'

'There were many men,' he says.

'There always were men, true,' I say.

I tell him about the men until he says that I must stop. It makes him ill with jealousy, he says.

'With you it's different,' I say. 'I have never yet loved somebody, I have never been someone else's. Those were

169

always strange affairs and I was someone who was being kept a secret. And I left it like that. It was right that way. But with you it's true, real.'

'I've been dreaming of that my entire life, of something real. Reality is staggeringly true and yet it remains highly unattainable. I always have the feeling that it isn't so, the way it is, that there's something awry. Reality always emerges hand in hand with something that enfeebles it, renders it unreal with something mendacious and false. Art has that quality, too, it truly is what it is and yet it is something else. Very difficult.'

'Your sculptures are about that, too, according to me.'

'They are?'

'What did you have in mind. What effect did you want to have on the people who saw your work?'

'In fact something like a sense of reality, but this I don't even have myself. The odd thing was that with the sculptures I wanted to achieve that they stopped looking at my sculptures and would learn to see true existence as it is. We cannot perceive reality. We actually see through language and through art and we don't see what is there.'

Lucas came and Lucas went. When he left I would stay behind and wouldn't know what to do with myself. I missed him. I no longer knew how to be satisfied with having my own eyes, ears and mouth. I wasn't sufficient unto myself. Each time I was out of my mind with fear, afraid that he wouldn't come back.

But Lucas returned each time. Not least to make it clear to me that it was indeed never certain that he would come back again.

'I wouldn't mind being inside you,' I say, 'like an amoeba or some kind of disease which over time you begin to love.'

170

'Is it a law of true love,' I ask Lucas, 'that you are together and then you part again?'

'I don't know. Perhaps I, too, have never truly been someone else's.'

'The choreography of love is a cruel one. I don't like it. Attract and repel, who ever laid down that it has to be this way?'

'Maybe it could be done differently. Perhaps it's because of me, because I always hold back a touch.'

'So why don't you stop holding back?'

'I do love you really, or how should I put it ...'

'I know.'

'But not enough, perhaps.'

First, I lose my appetite. I become thin. When I see food, displayed in shop windows or on the market, I feel sick. The thought of having to chew on something, to have to grind up something with my teeth, is unbearable. Smells of food are abhorrent to me.

I drink and I smoke. I feel how empty I am inside and it reminds me of hunger, but this is hunger which asks to remain unassuaged. The hunger must hollow me out, cleanse, digest everything that's still inside there. Nothing can get in from outside through my mouth, it is unthinkable and unnecessary. Lucas is enough.

I do not care what it is. There is nothing to think about. I don't need to understand myself. I want to understand Lucas.

Then I lose handbags, purses full of money, my pen, my Borsalino, books and clothes.

I'm proud of it. I'm proud that I am losing.

When he shakes me from my sleep the sobbing simply continues, just like that. My face is wet with tears.

'You were crying in your sleep. You were howling like a

wounded dog, very loudly. It woke me up. What's up then, darling?'

I don't recall a dream, no images, nothing. I am surprised and sad.

'I don't know.'

'I'm not making you happy,' he says, and he lets go of me abruptly.

'Yes you are,' I say, 'it makes me very happy, this too, the sorrow. It comes along with you, with happiness. But the sorrow, you can do nothing about the sorrow. It's not because of you. It was there already.'

'It's as if I'm not getting a past with you, Lucas. We've been together for a year already, but each time we've been apart for just a short while it's as if in your solitude you've rendered time nil, as if you've decided to go because there's been nothing to stay for. That's when I see from your face that the desolation has crept back into it. In that short period of absence you've made yourself alone again. It hurts to see it, in your eyes, in what hovers around you. Each time you destroy our past again, the days we are together and you say that you're happy with me.'

'I don't believe I can do it, Marie, what you want. It's too high for me, too absolute. It can't last anyway, so much love from you, that's indeed what I think each time. When I go out of the door here I think every time that it's over and I won't ever get back in. I'll be losing you anyway.'

'I'd actually prepared myself for eternity, you know.'

'You're good for me, Marie.'

'You're good for me, too, Lucas.'

'No, I'm not good for you. If things go on like this there'll be nothing left of you.'

One evening he gets up, brusquely, with anger in his movements. He stomps off to the kitchen. I hear him rattling with pots and pans, butter hisses in the pan. A moment later he resolutely puts a plate of food down in front of my nose. Meat and vegetables.

'You must eat something,' he says.

I don't dare to refuse. I eat. With regret, I feel the emptiness disappear, feel how I become filled up and how I lose my strength. After that, I'm washed out.

'Will you please never do that again,' I say to Lucas, later on in bed, 'giving me something to eat when I don't want to eat. There are different ways of showing that you love me.'

'We barely have space to walk in your house. You keep everything because you think of each thing that one day you might transform it into a sculpture, of every unread book you think it contains the truth which will give the decisive turn to your life. You mortgage the future, and the emptiness of today continues. Your life is a permanent postponement. You talk about meanings but you defer the giving of meaning each time. With regard to us, too.

'You collect but possibilities and all those possibilities which still have to be realised make you restless and unhappy. They're becoming ever more numerous, more things and more books. They're lying there just waiting for you and remain worthless for as long as you do not touch them.'

'You want to change me.'

'No, darling, you're good enough for me. I want to make you happy. According to me, you yourself are the one who wants to change.'

'Yes, I do still want to change. But why, in fact?'

'Because you don't think yourself good enough and you

long to be good.'

The day I faint for the first time and the bleeding starts coincides with the day that Guido de Waeterlinck rings and asks me to come and work at the university as a philosopher.

The choice seems a dramatic one to me, as if I must choose for life and against love. I have a month's time. I bleed and doubt for a month.

When the month has passed I wake up Lucas in the middle of the night. I am fearful.

'I don't know any more,' I say to Lucas.

'At last,' says he.

Chapter VII

THE PSYCHIATRIST

Monday, September 15, 1986 – 2.00 pm

Doctor, I'm a sham.

You listen. It is your job to hear something in my words which I am not saying, which I'm withholding from you, whether I want to or not, isn't it?

You fetch the truth from behind my stories, the truth I do not have. In fact, you're quite similar to a professional reader.

It is good to maintain our distance. If you don't mind, I should prefer to keep things formal between us. Feel free to address me on first name terms. You have to be stronger than me. I'm in trouble.

Just to be perfectly clear about this, I had already heard about you. You are Daniel's father and you were the psychiatrist of Lucas Asbeek, the man I loved, I love. Lucas was the end. In Lucas I flunked my last chance. I failed in that love.

I'm an impossible person. There's no living with me.

Everything meshes. It alarms me, the connection between

the signs. It's too much: too many themes, too many motives, too many masters, too many languages, incomplete tales, contradictions, all too much of everything. It now goes on outside me. So where am I to begin and where is it leading to? Nowhere, to confusion in the soul.

I no longer feel myself to be the organiser of this coincidence. Someone is playing with me, someone other than myself. He's trying to get something into my skull, but what is it in heaven's name?

He, oh yes, it's a *he*. He's rather divine, and powerful above all – otherwise one couldn't do such a thing.

I don't know where to begin.

I will begin with the astrologer, that's what I call him, consistently. He's dead. His real name was Miel, Miel van Eysden. He fell into a ravine. He was a friend of mine. Can I say such a thing? Yes, he was a friend.

Of late, I often have to think of him. He had something with figures and with the stars, of course. Every day he'd manage to see the figure thirty-three pop up somewhere, and every day he checked in his books of figures why that which had occurred that day had occurred. Then the world would add up and he'd be able to explain his suffering. I understand him better now. He's as mad as a hatter – I thought so at times even then – but something similar is happening in my head now. Discovering all sorts of messages.

Today is the day of the Seven Sorrows of the Holy Virgin Marie, moreover it's a Monday and the number of your house is the figure that has chased me into the world. On and on. And what does it mean?

I wouldn't have a clue which book has to clarify to me in hindsight why things are happening to me the way they are

176

now. In fact, I have the feeling more often of ending up in the books I myself, personally, have written earlier – in my head, that is. And I want out. I want out, outside the boundaries of this book.

This – a thing I certainly must say to you – this is also what worries me and harries me. It is as if my life has everything in common with literature. It resembles it so. In literature, too, the meanest word has meaning and everything is connected with everything else, as is the case in my life, now. And I always did think, before it engulfed me, that I was doing it myself, laying the connections between diverse incidents, that this was a way of extending beauty to life, and meaning. How else are you to make it meaningful?

However, no literature comes out of me. It begs the question whether it is indeed a good thing that my life resembles a book. I don't want a romantic life at all, if only I'm capable of writing a book. That's a must. Now. It's time.

You do occasionally hear about writers who only started a book after they had been to a psychiatrist, but on the other hand you also hear stories at times of people who were already busy writing or painting and who then went to a psychiatrist and since that time have never put pen to paper or held a brush, ever again. If that's the way things stand with me, doctor, then you must leave my soul be and tell me now – then I'm going. I'll manage. I can take care of myself.

I want to become a person, someone with her own life and with eyes which themselves see things, in my own proper way, not in someone else's. And I should also wish to hear words well up in me, entirely my own. The filth of others is everywhere, like a crust encasing language, like a mist

177

before my eyes, eyes that look like they've been made from soiled glass. I really *can't* see anything. I muddle everything up, I mix categories: man-woman, literature-reality, truth-lie, and there is nothing within me that can act as an umpire by saying to the one: you're not what you seem to be, and to the other: you're the one, you are true, you are what you are and you're the one I choose for.

I cannot bear those equivocal goings-on, all those ambiguities: they make me bloody miserable.

Things are not going well with me.

Perhaps indeed I was a person, once. I cannot remember. Are you born a person? Are you already something then, innately, when you're lying there in your cradle and they haven't yet sent your head into a spin with all their nonsense?

The nonsense. The words, ideas and opinions of others, their laws, their morality, their science, have intoxicated me. My spirit has been raped in fact. And I just let it happen, invited it: I was giving the glad-eye like blazes. He predicted this to me, the astrologer did. What was it he called me? A platonic whore, I believe, something to that effect.

I no longer know what is good and what evil. I want to heal, recover from the thoughts of others, from another's life.

I want to be good.

I'm becoming so tired of acquiring a character.

I always thought she ambushed someone, madness did. Not so. You seek her out, you invite her, you give her admission and you even observe, tense, how you let her muck about with you a bit, what she can achieve in you. It's a trying-out, a mock battle, a wait-and-see how far you dare to let yourself go, how mad you dare to become. But the other in you, the one controlling everything and looking after you when necessary, that one's weakened yet remains present.

To go mad is to lose your senses completely, I thought, but this is not true. Senses by the cart-load here.

I damn well know the way things are looking for me.

It's a con. I think it's the so-manieth attempt to get on to the scent of truth, this going mad is. Only this time I have staked myself on it.

I have an encyclopaedic thirst for knowledge; I have sought it everywhere, I have had many masters. You are the master in retrieving the meaning of this, such a monologue.

The nuisance only is that I don't really believe in it, in the truth of my tale, in an ultimate meaning, not even now that it's about *me* and I have to gabble myself back to health here and I expect from you the impossible.

I say *she*, indeed I do. Madness is a woman.

Do you think it has any meaning, the way I play fast and loose with the gender of words? Are you reading something into that?

Our time is limited. I am thirty, we have but an hour and the sun is busy disappearing to boot.

My Sun is in the first House. That's a law. I ought to know who I am. That's the interpretation of the law. Such are the things in my head and they're no use to me, zero, zilch. Bother? Sure.

When I fall I shall weep with happiness, it popped into my mind, again and again. Beckett. You can long for the fall, for the ceasing to learn, getting stuck, stop developing yourself. Musil.

I'm not alone, not for a second.

Two weeks ago some unknown person picked me up off the street. I was cycling along the canals, in the direction of the Dam. I looked at the houses lining the canal and became ever more miserable. They've been made by people and people die but those houses continue to stand there. That's what I thought and at that moment I thought it all-encompassing and very tragic. On one of the bridges I suddenly saw a young punk. They're very recognisable. Their hair stands on end, they wear horrifically tight trousers, leather jackets with words painted on them, and tall, clumsy army-boots. He wasn't much older than fourteen, had an expensive camera with a long lens in his hands, and trippingly he chased after a pigeon with it. He wanted to capture that pigeon in an image, you see, and as I saw this, the punk himself distilled in my mind into a symbol. It was one of something impossible and painful. For, that boy must die even so and the pigeon will die, as will I, I who see and imagine all this. There's no point whatsoever in photographing that pigeon. You will not escape death. The photograph will, perhaps. I crashed into an elevated bit, just like that, and I fell. I was lying there and didn't mind staying like that for ever. A passer-by helped me to my feet, a man, a Frenchman he was. He supported me and said to me in a voice full of concern: '*Mais petite*'. *Mais petite.* Then I put my arms around his neck and clutched him tight. I said to him something like: 'help me, love me, never leave me ever, protect me, save me, I am dying.' To a perfect stranger.

He did not understand those words, but he was very caring. I saw I was making him anxious, too – blew my nose, thanked him.

The incident with the punk was decisive. You, too, are a stranger. I should like to say the same to you.

It's quite something, asking for help. Curiously enough, it's – no, never mind.

180

I'm sorry I'm talking such gibberish and cannot bring structure to all I have to tell you. Back home, when I was alone, it all seemed so coherent to me, as if it was watertight, an orderly tale that added up, with a clear beginning and an end, one that would be of some use to you.

How long have we still got?

May I start afresh once more?

Doesn't it make you terribly tired, having to listen to me for so long?

At times I have the feeling as if I've rumbled the world's game, as if I see how everything is in its proper place and how everything has its time and its own proper necessity, and how likewise their own life is the only thing that people have because it's the focal junction for everything that occurs in your life, and if you don't have your own junction then you're without anything, for then every event is nondescript, without connection, just an event, without value, a worthless passing incident that might as well not have happened, a dangling thread, meaningless. Only people with a life of their own are capable of seeing a story in what life in fact is, who beneath the gruesome differences of every minute listen to the unity, the unity of their story, only such people can be happy.

Doctor, I am intensely happy, but I can no longer cope with my happiness.

I should like to preach to the world, teach people how they must listen to that language which is obscured by the incidents in their lives. Then they themselves can also become people again, people who liberate the world from its stupid pointlessness, from the needless, silent presence of the world. Otherwise your life's a misery, surely, if you're not capable of that?

I pity us people. Nietzsche disapproves of pity; to Schopenhauer all love is pity, so what on earth are you

181

meant to be doing then, for heaven's sake? Is it good or is it bad to feel pity? Well?

I feel very alone.

I don't know how to make myself understood.

The essence of things doesn't exist, doctor, not without us, in any case. What we make of it is what it'll be, nothing else.

But what's the case with people themselves, then? Are you, as a human being, born with an essence?

Take it that people fare the same way that things do, that in themselves people are nothing either, that's to say nothing at all. Gruesome thought and therefore probably true. Then people are just as interdependent of one another as things are dependent on us, then we can only be what another makes of us. Then we can only mean something when others have the preparedness, the love, to give us meaning in their tale. Then we are characters by force of necessity in someone else's story, and other than that, in our loneliness, we amount to nothing at all, we're insignificant, meaningless, silent and superfluous things. We are at the mercy of others' clemency, of their hackwork. Those of us involved in this can only stand by, helplessly.

Some people become mild with love, and compliant; not me. I became wild and went on the offensive. The harder I fought, the more loving I was. I don't get it at all.

I devour people but others devour me as well, most definitely. Love has scared me rigid.

I can't make things out too well any more. You must help me to gain clarity again and to learn to separate the goats from the sheep.

What I mean is this: when your own life is the only thing

that makes your life worthwhile and it's also the only instrument by which you can give meaning to life, and if you also realise that your life is still at the mercy of others and only they can make you, then that's a terrible thought, isn't it?

Do you understand what I mean to say?

Why am I sitting here? How did I manage to end up here? I have a talent for happiness, doctor, honest, always did, never doubted it. I've always felt myself to be blessed, gifted with the capacity to make of life a beautiful life, no matter how it goes. It has always had beauty.

I must withdraw from people and remain in my house to protect myself against events, for the moment I set foot outside the door, the world storms up to me like a devil-may-care dog and I have no defence whatsoever, the most diminutive thing I see touches me like something important and gives me sorrow or fierce happiness while in fact I should like to keep it safe, release the event from its place and time, liberate it by incorporating it in my tale and giving it meaning.

I have read too many books. Too much is happening in my head.

At times I am dead-beat from seeing. It's quite simply unhealthy how happy I am. I wear myself down.

Is this normal?

Does it all still add up?

So, what I actually want to say is that individual incidents do not exist. That which is individual and alone, and doesn't fit in anywhere, has no meaning. We must rescue things and people, liberate them from their meaninglessness, over and over again, ever afresh. The problem then is that I cannot rescue myself. I am the only one who is individual; I cannot give myself meaning. I find it unpleasant to be so empty and without meaning myself.

I wanted to help Lucas, to comfort him and mediate between him and him, between him and the enemy of himself also inside him. He is so disorganised and divided inside, two in one, and then I'm keeping numbers down on the conservative side. He lets in much doubt. He had never been loved enough. I believed, by loving him a lot, to be able to let him become more real so that he would dare to come down, both feet on the ground, and then to be striding alongside me, full feather, here in this terrestrial world, preferably permanently so. I felt myself to be his bride.

What I absolutely must tell you about the matter is this: for the first time in my life I believed I understood what the nature of a woman is, what womankind is predestined to.

I wanted to bear him a son.

All at once I also understood those songs on the radio. *You make me feel like a natural woman.* I no longer thought them ridiculous, sang along with them full-voice, silly goose. Yet I understood, at the time, that it is intended that women bear children and that they shouldn't get any ideas in their pretty little heads, for the rest is either nonsense or it does not belong to the domain of women.

A woman who writes enters upon the domain of men. She abandons her own means of granting herself meaning via another, and grabs for the means of men: that pen, those letters, weapons of impotence.

Men also write books in order to seduce women into loving them, if only in their heads, and when a woman writes a book she thinks that with this she can seduce the man into loving her, but men take to their heels faced with writing women. It's not at all the intention that a woman should do what men are good at. I was already mistaken in this, much earlier on. I believed that boys liked girls who were just as they, the boys. So I was an even fiercer Winnetou, a tougher soldier, more implacable in fighting, rougher, more cruel, more reckless.

But boys don't like things which resemble them at all. They like real girls who make themselves up and giggle and who talk about girls' things, who do everything I once forbad myself to do.

I have mixed up desire and desirability mightily, being and having as well. I became the same as the one who I thought desirable to have, to be desired by myself. I was the one who so badly had to be someone.

Is that what I continued my studies for, for so long: in order to discover the truth of clichés?

I wanted Lucas and in order to have him, I had to be a woman. That love was more of a taking-away than an adding-to. To tear down, unlearn, crack, lose, to lose much especially. Water, flesh, fat, phrases, tricks, habits, checking, waste paper, dreams, losing my nonsense. With Lucas, I agreed with myself, I was light and simple, an easy sum of possibilities which only needed to be added on to him. It was clear: he was the most important thing in my life, he was at the top of the hierarchy, elevated above all and sundry: even so, I knew what I had to choose for. For him.

I cannot bear doubt. I cannot horse-trade with fate, make compromises about the most important thing that awaits me to be done in life, bargaining with it and serving several gods at once. It's either one or the other. I have to choose. It's not so much that I am not divided over this, I quite simply refuse to be divided, full stop.

When I was with him and the desire to write would arise in me again, I experienced it as treachery and I could bawl my head off about Lucas because I was afraid not to have loved him enough for just a moment.

In the end, he could not bear my love. Who could?

185

It affected his self-hate, he said, and that he did not love himself enough to be able to love me.

Since when does this stark-staring bromide have us in its thrall? Which brain-dead nutcase has been stamping this into people's heads, that they must first love themselves before they'll be able to love someone else? It is the most preposterous, the most hare-brained, the most cruel law *ever* and it rules the twentieth century. This is mind-boggling nonsense. You have to love someone else and someone else has to love you, so you shouldn't still have to do that yourself as well: that's impossible. Just who does love himself without being loved by another? No one, surely? Ah yes, of course, a handful of monomaniacal idiots with nine assertiveness training-sessions under their belts. Quite.

I have such a longing for self-oblivion, for the one thing in my life to which I can devote myself, something other than myself. Higher and better.

I'm sorry. I had resolved to tell you everything, honestly and without diffidence but it's not to be done, telling you everything shamelessly as well as not lying.

To myself I seem to be terribly artificial, as if I have invented myself and have provided myself with a fictional character. And, one day, someone will come and demand something from me, something of myself. Then it will come to light that I have no such things to offer, none my own.

Monday, September 22, 1986 – 2.00 pm

By and by, the world has become so predictable, always the same old stuff. Perhaps I ought to say *my* world, *my* world has become predictable. I would like things to go differently for once, an encounter, for instance, but it always turns into the same old thing, and that it will turn out to be like this I know after a few minutes. I long for unpredictable events, for moments of which I do not know the plot in advance, for encounters with people of which I cannot predict instantly how they will run their course. The predictability of others makes me cold and indifferent. It is then as if I have no experiences. I even feel myself to be the organiser and producer of that which presents itself as being a coincidence.

Surely it's Jung who writes somewhere that fate is something you bring about in the world yourself? It is something which in fact takes place within you, a conflict. And if you don't take the trouble to realise that you are wrestling with such a conflict, how it's made up and what is actually embroiled with what, and this just goes on as if nothing's the matter at all, then the conflict moves to the outside world and assumes the form there of fate.

What then is my fate?

Fate: eternal repetitions, surely?

So I must ask myself what it is that is repeating itself all the time in my life, what it is that returns each time in the same form.

Encounters, men, I think: always the same story, except in Lucas' case. Lucas is a different chapter.

Men make the laws. By the laws they connect that which lies far apart, heaven and earth, body and soul, you know, the opposites. And then, their laws in hand, they read the world. You included. If this, then that. You such, therefore this. They read you like a book. I have listened to them, to their stories about the world, about myself especially. I have loved none of these men the way I loved Lucas, love Lucas. I don't believe either that any of those men loved

187

me, not truly.

Perhaps it was impossible. I wasn't in search of love. I sought those laws.

I was too available and, precisely because of that, inaccessible. I was a joker in the pack, without a fixed place, without a fixed shape, to be applied anywhere. They could make of me what they wanted, Queen of Hearts, Jack of Spades. No problem.

Lucas did not make me. With Lucas I was Marie, Queen of Hearts. I opened with Hearts and lost.

Men know a lot of the world and little of themselves. They spin entire networks between disparate things and sometimes they don't latch on to it that their knowledge is only a way of keeping their heads above water. I do. Behind the men stood other men and those were the men from whom they had learned the laws. I listened and ate. They always gave me food, the men did.

When they had told me their story, I would tell them something about themselves, mostly about the sins they'd kept back, then judge them more mildly than they could ever do themselves. I want to speak up for men. Someone has to forgive you for the fact that, in all your attempts to do things well, you make errors and commit clangers. This someone can only be a woman. Tell me, who doesn't ask forgiveness of a woman?

I love men. They are lonely.

In fact we all want the same thing: to become saintly, divine. But it does not fall to man to be divine. A human being is human and that's plenty hard enough. Since they brought down God from above and attributed a place to him in the heart of man, things have gone horribly wrong. God belongs above, below, everywhere: outside of man, in any case. You can desire the divine, strive after it, and if you do it right you become a little bit saintly at best.

188

The men wanted me to listen to them and to forgive them. They were satisfied with little and I was able to give them that little bit, only just.

You know I do not want this, a psycho-analytical interpretation. You have allowed me to keep silent about that, about the true father, mother, brothers. You have promised to spare me certain words because you know that I don't think those are good words with which to interpret a story. We would not utter them.

You know we will be together a short while. I won't remain long with you. No longer than is necessary for this story.

I am not after understanding why I have become the one I am. When I said to you that I'm a sham, I wasn't lying.

For as far back as I can remember I have wanted to become *it*. In fact my memories only start from the moment I was able to read the first words. What happened before then I have forgotten, radically. I learned to read, I learned to remember in words and from that time onward I wanted to become someone the words came from. All I have done since has to do with this desire. I wished to assuage it and escape from it at the same time: very odd. I continued my studies for seven years and have only occupied myself with that question: why. Why do I want to become this? What is this writing, literature? What use is it?

I can't stand it that this has to be a fate. There's nothing more to understand about a fate. It is what it is. You can never justify a fate. A choice you can.

On the quiet, I still hope for an answer, for something from outside, something that changes me into someone who is capable of making the choice without doubting. That something, that is the ultimate initiation. From you, too, I

expect this.
But it's feeble and preposterous.
This event will never take place.

That which I tell you is no history of becoming. It is more of a history of un-becoming, of becoming impersonal. Is that possible? I believe I can't stand having a personal life. The thought that experiences, adventures, feelings are only experienced like this by *me*: with such a thought I cannot live. When I experience something, I see in it something that transcends myself. If I don't see that, I might as well not experience it: my day is pointless then. I like to see everything big.
The law is impersonal.
Laws apply to everyone, I thought.

You must render yourself dead in order to be able to write. I believe that that's the thing, that it's that kind of a way of life. I believe the astrologer was right and that I can only be in society through something other than myself, by myself being absent.
It is true: I hate paradoxes, I loathe paradoxes. Yet it is the only law I run up against in fact. The paradox is within the law itself.

You think me cerebral, abstract and cryptic.
Next time I will be more modest and tell you an orderly tale. It has to be possible to silence that voice inside me, surely. The end is a monologue, but the only point to a monologue is to have it come to an end by itself, peace, silence, wordlessness.

Monday, September 29, 1986 – 2.00 pm

Life was a good deal simpler when I still believed in God. If that's the way you want it, I still do believe in God, but He is no longer quite what He was. God will not tolerate meaning all kinds of things and becoming the great stop-gap in a piece of which you no longer are able to get the words to make sense. So that's what He is now: a stop-gap for the absurd. I know I cannot do that to Him, somehow. He has His pride, too, you know, God has.

It went wrong between us when I laid my hands on that paperback of lectures by Mr Jean-Paul Sartre, about existentialism.

I was almost fourteen.

The village where I was born is beautiful and the people who live there are Catholics. When you have been born a Catholic you know no better, for some time at least.

It's not bad at all being a Catholic. We had lots of celebrations and few laws. You came to hear some rules from the priest and you learned these by heart. They were simple and easy to remember. You could not imagine that these were rules which only should apply to Catholics, for of course you understood that it would be chaos on earth in no time should the entire world not live by them.

Once you have rules in your head you can't get them out of there again so easily.

I believed it could do no harm.

What would one do without rules?

The Procession of the Sacrament was the finest.

Then the women from the village would go, very early in the morning, to the fields, together. They would bring along cane baskets. The plants would be in full flower.

Alongside one another and talking busily about the

191

things the women in the village would always talk about, they would stand bent over the soil and with their bare hands rip the colourful petals from the buds. In their baskets they gathered a harvest of colour, the blue of the cornflower, the red of the poppy, the lilac of clover.

You can't pull up fern fronds with your bare hands. The women in charge of the greenery all had a pair of scissors on them.

I was eleven already when I was allowed to come along with the women. I could do the picking alright, that wasn't the thing, but I could not join in with their talk. I didn't understand the things the women were talking about when they spoke with one another. I understood more of the story of Christ's resurrection.

In the main they talked about other women.

I was excited and was looking forward to the procession.

I was the Angel of Hope.

I would have preferred to be the Angel of Love but they only had a green dress in my size.

I never did become very tall.

At ten o'clock we went back to the village and sprinkled petals on the asphalt. The road surface became a carpet of colour. Pity really that everybody had to tread on it with their feet but you didn't think of such things, then. Beauty was good.

As we went along the roads, sowing to all sides, we passed the men who were busy placing the white-and-yellow flags along the side of the street and the houses where the other women were busy building their altar. Beneath an open window tables were being placed in a stairs-like configuration and covered in spotless, starched white sheets. The rich had damask sheets, most people had ordinary cotton ones on which they had embroidered little figures by hand.

Candlesticks with burning candles, vases of flowers and statues of saints were placed on the altar. The one who loved Joseph most had Joseph outside and one who had more truck with Mary, The Burning Heart or with St Francis, now allowed this to be seen, too. You could get to know people better this way.

My eldest brother was an acolyte, the youngest a shepherd and I was among the angels. The eldest went his own way, he was allowed into the sacristy. My younger brother and I walked together to the monastery where we were to change our clothes. He didn't really want to any more. Not because of God. He didn't like dressing up.

The shepherds were downstairs with the friar. I had to go up some stairs to an upper floor where the nuns were looking after the angels.

It smelled there of floor polish and chicken stock.

When I came in they'd always be bustling, busy with the archangel. She had to appear an hour sooner than the ordinary angels, for each year it was quite a to-do to get the wings fixed on. One time, the wings of the archangel came loose during the procession and they dropped down in front of the feet of the toddlers who were connected by ribbons to her. One child tripped over the wings and remained a cripple ever after.

Enough to almost topple you from your faith when you hear such tales.

The archangel is the most beautiful of all. She has a pale-blue dress and lots of extras. A halo, wings, and ribbons with children attached.

But to become an archangel you had to be one metre seventy, at least, and I wasn't.

An older boy from the village went to school in town and he gave me the book. As he did this, he said that I probably wouldn't understand it anyway.

You should never say things like that to me.

I read it at night in bed. Somehow, somewhere I suspected a connection between the incomprehensible and the forbidden. Rightly so.

I don't know whether at that time I still believed in God. I only know that after that time I did my best no longer to believe.

What I understood was this: God doesn't exist and this is why you must make a choice yourself and bear the responsibility for it.

I thought it not a little brave of Mr Sartre, writing that He doesn't exist, just like that.

You never can tell.

That year I no longer turned up as the Angel of Hope.

I was an existentialist.

I knew the route of the procession. I had chosen to set myself up at the foot of the monumental steps. The road slopes at that point and the steps lead to the church, on top of Mount Odilia. From there I would be able to see the procession way ahead of time and prepare myself fully on the spot for the deed.

Things have been different.

There was a time when I spent entire mornings in and around the church. I attended all masses and afterwards I tended the neglected graves in the churchyard. Back home they were worried about my zeal and in all kinds of ways they attempted to divert my attention to keep me away from church.

So I went even more often and stayed away for longer.

I encountered quite some resistance from the parish priest as well. He would always pull my hair when passing me on the steps. 'Hey, whitey,' he'd then hiss between his teeth, for I had white hair.

Ever since I had asked him whether I could become an acolyte and later on a priest, like him, I was under the impression that he greeted me more roughly. It hurt, sometimes.

The priest wasn't into girls that much, I think.

So I went and sat each day in such a place that he'd be able to see me from the altar.

You had to be prepared to make some sacrifice.

In the distance rose the sonorous sound of the brass band and then the rhythmical praying of the men and the women. One prayed first in a loud voice and then the rest joined in. The sound came to me in waves. I suddenly felt sick at heart.

I did ask Him what on earth had got into me, and I asked for strength as well to bring the deed to completion. Afterwards, I wished most to wipe out those thoughts, for I, too, quite understood that it's not fitting for an existentialist to bother Him any longer.

The procession approached. The priest walked in front with the monstrance held aloft. The golden aureole caught the clear morning sunlight which glanced off, reflected in all directions. Behind went the acolytes with the bier upon which stood the statue of Saint Odilia. She is our patron saint. She can make the blind see again.

The voices of the praying populace got louder and louder. To left and right of me people began to kneel and bow their heads.

That's the way it should be.

195

Folding my hands, loosely in front of my tummy, was the first concession. I tried to recall some sentences from the book but the only things that would come to mind were individual words: man, freedom, desolation, choice, responsibility, acts.

The monstrance glinted at less than ten metres distance from me and the procession continued on its way. Everyone around me had knelt down. I was the only one still standing upright. Perhaps no one will even notice, I even thought. I'm still so small.

Before I made the second concession and closed my eyes, I just recognised my grandfather's beautiful face, immediately behind the bier with the statue. He was one of the oldest in the village and he walked with a stick from which dangled a burning lantern. He was now already at such an age that he had penetrated to the front row of enlightened ones.

I would have wished to have spared him the scene, believe you me.

Devout, but straight as a rod, I stood among the kneeling ones, to wait till all had passed, until the murmuring noise would ebb away and the cadence of prayers would wind its way up the mountain, far away from me.

It took an eternity.

Suddenly the sound halted immediately in front of me. I cast up my eyes and looked into the face, distorted with rage, of the priest. He turned his full width toward me and raised the monstrance high above his head.

'Kneel,' he hissed, 'kneel before the Most Holy, whitey!'

I did not bend my knees, I crashed down on to them.

I wanted to pray for forgiveness, I believe, but I no longer knew who was to grant me that forgiveness: God, my grandfather or Mr Sartre.

196

Monday, October 6, 1986 – 2.00 pm

I'll be off in a moment. I have nothing more to say to you. I'm taking my leave of you. It has been good. I have heeded your request and written the story down. Then I was outrageously happy for a moment, first for a long time. This must be it then – so be it.

It was not so much your analysis which tipped the balance, for I don't know whether I agree with your interpretations or not, rather it was the miracle of your being able to give meaning to it, to the story itself.

It's for you – I have put my signature to it and I leave it behind here. I do have a copy myself.

I couldn't think of a name for the tale. A title can never match the contents any way.

Amsterdam, June 1990